A WORLD BENEATH THE SEA

"There's a world below this world, Barry," he said. "The real world. Look."

With a single giant flicker, the sea lit up. Far below there was a vast winding valley. It was mottled like a lizard, and immense terraced cliffs rose from the foothills, their castle-like tops facing each other. There were canyons beyond, and swarming in and out were millions of fish. The walls and terraces were of every color — purple, green, tangerine. Ahead was a mountain range, and the nearest peak was shining turquoise. There was a forest on its crest. . . .

UNDER
PLUM LAKE

Lionel Davidson

Drawings by Muriel Nasser

BANTAM BOOKS
TORONTO · NEW YORK · LONDON · SYDNEY · AUCKLAND

UNDER PLUM LAKE
*A Bantam Book / published by arrangement with
Alfred A. Knopf, Inc.*

PRINTING HISTORY
Knopf edition published October 1980
*Originally published in Great Britain by Jonathan Cape Limited,
London*
Bantam Spectra edition / September 1983
2nd printing . . . October 1985
All rights reserved.
Copyright © 1980 by Manningford Ltd.
Cover art copyright © 1985 by Victoria Poiser.
*This book may not be reproduced in whole or in part, by
mimeograph or any other means, without permission.*
*For information address: Alfred A. Knopf Inc.,
201 East 50th Street, New York, NY 10022.*

ISBN 0-553-25372-7

Under the Mountains

GOING DOWN

I went down again last night. I go every night now. It's August again, the same time of year, and I know it can still all happen again. If I try hard enough, I can make it happen.

The difficulty is remembering. So much is missing, and even what I remember seems crazy and out of order. It's like when you are very young and wakened at night and taken somewhere, and afterwards can't tell if it really happened or if you dreamed it.

I know I didn't dream this. I couldn't dream Mount Julas or the Glister Deep or Plum Lake. I couldn't even imagine them. They're unimaginable. So they're there, and the knowledge hasn't all drained out of me, as Dido said it would, like when you're born or when you die.

I've got to hang on to that.

But I've got to hang on to all of it.

I've got to put down what I remember.

I'll do it every day. I'll lock it in my case. Then I'll lock the cupboard, too. I don't want anyone finding it till I'm finished. Then if it looks crazy I'll —

3

I won't say now what I'll do.

I know they're talking about me. Dad says he thinks a doctor ought to look at me again. I am not having a doctor look at me. I will act normally. I'll talk more at meals and listen to what they say and answer better. All the time now I'm remembering more. And I have the time. They don't disturb me in the mornings. (I had a bad year at school. I couldn't concentrate after what happened last year, so I have extra holiday tasks.)

Because they don't disturb me, nobody knows if I'm in my room or not. Often I'm not. I go down in the mornings, too. I go down the cliff.

I know the sea way, but the cliff is better. I'm out of sight there. Sometimes, going down, I wonder if Dido is watching. I'll bet he is. I know he is.

It's 380 feet down the cliff. It isn't dangerous unless the weather is bad. I wouldn't do it in bad weather. After the gale last year it was three days before they found me in the cave. Not that I was in it for three days. Where I was . . .

Well, I'll save that.

I'll definitely keep this locked up.

I can see now it looks confused. I'd better get it clearer. I'll make that the first job. I'll get it clear.

A FACE I
COULDN'T SEE

Polziel, Cornwall, August 4.

'll give the facts. I'll give all my details.
I'm Barry Gordon. I'm thirteen. I have two sisters,
Sarah, aged seventeen, and Annie, nine.

This is a house on a cliff. It's a wreck, really.

We came here for the first time last year. Dad
rented it then but he's buying it now. It is cheap
because no one wants it. It's only for summers. He is
putting in electricity and a bathroom. Last year it
just had oil lamps and a cooker that worked on coal.

Actually, it's great.

The walls are crooked because the ground has
sunk. I have the attic, and that's crooked, too. It's all
pretty terrific, and the only blot on the scene is
Annie, so I'll start with her. She is skinny and small,
a fantastic liar. She tells tales and gets people into
trouble. They say she is "imaginative," and they're
right. She imagines so many things she scares her-
self. She won't go to bed without a night light.

Any scare story that is going, she is the first to
hear it. Last year, in Seele, she was the first to hear of

the village that fell in the sea. Seele is the fishing village across the bay. The people there are idiots. They believe anything. They say the village that fell in the sea was ours.

They say it fell in the sea because it was cursed. (There is no village here. There was once supposed to be one where the line of rocks stands out in the bay.) They say the people in it were "wreckers," who attacked ships and robbed them, and that no one ever discovered where they hid the stuff they stole.

The crazy people believe the villagers are still at the bottom of the sea and that their ghosts come up and put lights out and haunt places. They believe if you sail past the rocks on Sunday, you hear church bells ringing under water. It's true their boats won't go near the place. The people won't even come this side of the bay by land.

When Annie heard of the ghosts coming up and haunting, she wouldn't go to bed even with a night light. She wouldn't go unless Sarah went with her. Just then she was being such a fantastic pest that most of the day I was stuck with her. Everywhere I went, she went. I couldn't go to the beach without her.

Our beach here is the best for miles. It's a narrow inlet with cliffs on both sides. Where the cliffs meet at the back (where the rock crumbles and slopes) is where you get down.

Last year the weather was so hot my mother and Sarah came down and swam some days. Mainly I was stuck with Annie, though.

She wouldn't swim out in the bay.

She wouldn't let me go alone, either, so I waited one day till my mother and Sarah came, and I went.

The cliffs on both sides stretch out a long way but the one at our side goes farthest. I couldn't see the west face of it from Seele. This was the face I wanted to see.

I'd better say now I get ideas on holiday. Usually, I get the idea I am going to find something about a place that no one has found before. The idea I had this time was that I would find where the wreckers hid their stuff. I thought they hid it in the cliff.

It looks dopey now I've put it, I can see that. Anyway, that was the one I had.

It was a long swim so I took it easy, and rested a few times, and finally turned the corner of the cliff, and there was the west face.

Right away, I saw it was a monster.

The giant wall of rock rose sheer from the sea.

Just above water level were three caves.

As I drew closer I saw they were some way above sea level. They were ten feet above.

Treading water I looked up. I could see there was no way up without a rope. There were no footholds, just razor edges of rock. The tide was coming in, but it wouldn't come in much more.

I was too near the sharp rocks so I backed off. I knew I mustn't stay long. The tide would be turning, and I couldn't swim back against it.

I stayed a bit longer, though.

The caves were in a line, dark ovals, about my own height. I thought I could see something in one of them. The sun was in my eyes, and the oval mouths shadowed. I knew there couldn't be anything useful there. Anything useful would have been taken long ago. Except just then I thought of something else. The people of Seele wouldn't come near this place.

No one else would risk a boat near the rocks, either. It might be that I was the only person for years to get this close.

The sea had developed a slow kind of heave, as if the tide was on the turn, so I went then.

I didn't rest on the way back. I rounded the cliff and struck out strongly for the shore. I saw my mother and Sarah and Annie standing at the water's edge, looking out to sea. They began waving as they saw me.

Even before I hit the beach I heard my mother shouting, "You bad boy! Where did you go?"

"Round the cliff for a swim," I said.

"You went right out of sight! Never let me see you do that again! Do you hear what I'm saying?"

"Yeah. Okay," I said.

I meant I heard what she was saying.

She didn't want to see me do it again.

Next day I made sure she didn't.

THE FACE AGAIN

I did it early, before anyone was up. As soon as I left the house I knew something was wrong. The weather had changed, and was heavy and grey. The tide wasn't right, either. It was coming in, but not enough. I'd be lower in the water and it would be harder to see into the caves.

Also, I had a feeling someone was watching.

I looked all round, but no one was watching.

I swam out. I didn't rest this time. I rounded the cliff, and there it was.

In the grey light the west face reared out of the sea like a skyscraper.

I saw now there was a bulge near the top, like a boil sticking out. There was a line of foam where the tide nudged the cliff.

The water was much lower, five feet lower.

I couldn't see anything in the caves.

There were the three black openings, and not even so much of them. They'd been oval before. They weren't oval now.

This was strange, and I bobbed around for a

while, trying to work it out. I bobbed close to the face, and then away. I thought maybe the sun had made them look different before. The sun, casting shadows, had made the mouths oval.

I swam farther to see if there was some other way up. I swam a couple of hundred yards, and grew uneasy. The enormous mass of grey sea was heaving slightly. I was like a fly on it. I couldn't see Seele. I couldn't see anywhere. Beyond the gigantic line of cliffs there was just the Atlantic.

I thought I'd better go.

I took a rest, and looked up, and saw the ledge.

I saw one ledge, and above it another, and above that one more.

They were narrow ledges, just ridges, but long and regular and made the cliff look like a piece of cheese that different people have been cutting. The cliff was a slatey kind that the sea hadn't rubbed smooth but had just broken off. It gave the ledges a sharp edge. The bottom one was four feet above my head.

I went closer and grabbed up at it.

It took a few grabs, but I managed it and began pulling myself up. Just as I made it, the edge broke and I fell back with two samples of rock in my hands.

I had a look at them in the water. They were flaky pieces of grey slate. One seemed red underneath and I turned it over curiously, and saw it wasn't the slate that was red but my hand. I'd cut it. It wasn't a bad cut, but the blood made me uneasier.

Again, I had a strange feeling someone was watching me.

I pushed off but felt myself panting from jumping out of the water, and thought I'd take a breather.

I lay on my back and took one, and right away saw the cave mouths were oval.

I couldn't believe it.

I screwed up my eyes and peered.

They were oval as eggs.

They hadn't been oval a few minutes ago. After a long look I saw why. The bases of the cave mouths projected. Looking up from directly below, from fifteen feet below, the line of the bases had cut across the ovals. They hadn't yesterday. But I'd been higher in the water yesterday. Sideways now, I could see how the bases projected. They projected like platforms.

Treading water I inspected them.

They seemed almost intended as platforms.

Not only that: beyond the first (the first as you rounded the cliff) there was a flat piece of rock that could be a step. It looked intended as a step.

It was a pace down from the step to the platform; except I couldn't see how you got to the step. There was no way down the cliff. It was a sheer drop.

All this was puzzling, and I floated round and puzzled till a few single heavy drops of rain began to fall, and I looked up and saw the sky was down on top of me. The air was like cotton wool, very still. A storm was coming.

I started back right away.

I peered in the caves as I passed. I couldn't see in, so I flung one of the pieces of rock in. It made a kind of clunk as if it had hit a piece of wood, and fell on the platform and dropped in the sea.

As it did so, two birds flew up and began circling in the air. They hadn't flown out of the cave. I couldn't see where they'd flown from.

I watched a moment, and threw the other piece. I

11

threw it higher and it struck above the cave, and half a dozen more birds flew up. A moment later so did another four, from higher still. The whole flock began swooping about me, angrily squawking.

I watched them, fascinated. They swooped and circled, and then flew back where they came from. They hovered a moment, and dropped out of sight. They did it one after the other, in a diagonal line up the cliff.

I followed the line of the diagonal down the cliff. It stopped at the step.

I felt strange suddenly. I felt excited. I knew I'd seen something important. I felt myself tingling as if there was a lot of electricity in the air, and there was, because the next moment the sea sizzled and turned white.

It was either rain or hail, and it came drilling at my head and face, blinding me.

I went into a racing crawl. I swam as fast as I could till I'd safely rounded the cliff.

I didn't make it a second too early. I'd barely entered the inlet before a gigantic wind blew in from the sea. It was as if a door had opened miles away and the gale rushed through. The sea developed a tremendous lurch, and the line of foam at the cliff began exploding as waves crashed there. Ahead, a long way ahead, through the blinding rain, I could see the beach glimmering. It was a weird greenish colour. As I looked, it gave a twitch and turned white and purple, and there was a sound like tearing cloth and a gigantic clap of thunder.

In the tremendous waves I was being tossed like a matchstick, unable to swim, unable to do anything. I tried to float. But there was no way of floating. Great walls of water crashed on me, plunging me down. Three times I managed to struggle to the surface and take a breath. But I was weakened and sick with panic. The fourth time as I came up, a white mountain of sea fell on me. I sank and sank, spinning feebly, in thunderous foam.

I thought: I am drowning now. This is how you drown. I am dying. There was sea water in my throat and nose. My eardrums were pounding. I thought, this is the end of everything. And an undercurrent caught me.

It spun me in a circle in the water. It thrust me up at great speed. I broke surface to catch the crest of another wave—not this time on top, but behind me.

It took me and threw me, in a series of sickening lunges, into twenty-foot troughs and twenty-foot peaks, racing towards the beach.

Huge forks of lightning lit up the beach again before I hit it. I hit it on my knees, and tried to stand, and was knocked over, and tried again, and was knocked over again, and began scrabbling up the wet sand on my stomach, and lay for a while, exhausted.

I felt battered and dizzy, but full of excitement, and I looked back at the white roaring sea and wanted to yell and dance.

I felt half mad with relief at being alive. But it wasn't only that. I had the same electric feeling I'd felt when I saw the birds disappearing on the cliff face.

I felt full of strange knowledge.

For one thing I thought I knew where the wreckers had hidden their stuff; and I also had an idea how to get there. There was a track on the cliff, and one end went to the caves. The other one had to be on the clifftop.

But still I felt strange. I felt watched.

And I was being watched, but not the way I felt. My father and Annie were on the clifftop. The little pest had woken in the storm and had found I wasn't in my room. So my father was waiting when I got back.

He said, "What did your mother say about swimming out there?"

I licked my lips. "She didn't want to *see* me do it," I said.

"Come here," he said.

He was breathing hard when he finished, and I was rubbing my behind.

"Maybe you'll get the idea from me," he said.

"Yes," I said.

"No swimming past the cliffs again."

"No."

"Or sneaking out early in the morning. A fine example to set your little sister!"

I could hear my little sister, breathing behind the door. She'd been listening, enjoying every minute.

I thought I'd settle her later.

THE FACE BY NIGHT

I've got to get the time right now. I've got to say how it happened. My father hadn't started his holiday then. He just came weekends. He came Friday night and went Sunday night.

He gave me the walloping Saturday morning, so I waited all weekend for him to go. The storm blew out during the weekend, but the weather stayed strange. It stayed grey and heavy.

This worried my mother because when it was time for him to go the tracks were still muddy and the roads unlit for miles.

"Don't worry," he said, and looked up at the sky. "In a couple of hours it will be bright as day."

I said, "Will it?"

"Yes. Full moon tonight." He looked up again and took a deep breath before climbing into the car.

I went back in the house with my stomach churning.

I said, "Can I have the flashlight?"

"Why do you want the flashlight?" my mother said.

"I thought I'd get coal for the morning."

"Very thoughtful. It's in my bedroom drawer. See it goes back there."

I got the flashlight and went out and shovelled coal.

The flashlight didn't go back in the drawer.

Later Annie went to bed, so Sarah had to go with her.

"I think I'll read awhile," my mother said.

"I think I'll go to bed," I said.

My stomach was still churning as I creaked up the stairs. I'd got the flashlight under my pullover and an oil lamp in my hand. I shut the attic door and looked out the window.

It wasn't bright as day yet. I hoped Dad was right.

In another way, I hoped he wasn't.

It seemed crazy going down the cliff at night.

Annie would keep an eye on me all day, though.

I thought I'd consider it, and lay down on the bed; and the next thing I knew my mother was calling me. She seemed to have done it once or twice already, and she was doing it in a hushed voice, not to wake the others.

She said, "Barry—did you take the flashlight?"

I kept quiet. I knew she wouldn't come and wake me just for the flashlight.

I heard her door close and the bedsprings creak.

I got up and looked out the window.

It was bright moonlight.

I licked my lips and felt for the flashlight and began creeping downstairs.

"Barry?" my mother said.

I froze.

"Is that you, Barry?"

16

I turned and went back up, two at a time, keeping to the wall side, where the stairs creaked less, and re-entered my room and stood cursing in the dark. I'd have to wait till she was asleep.

In the light of the flashlight I looked at my watch, and then looked again.

One o'clock! I'd been "considering" it for two hours. There was no question of waiting till she was asleep now. She couldn't sleep for hours the night my father left. It would have to be now. It would have to be by the window.

I had another look out of the window.

The attic faced back. The storm porch was just below, with the coal pile under it. There was a sloping slate roof, held up by a wooden post.

I went backwards out the window, and hung on till I felt the roof below, and went down the slates. There was a rainwater gutter at the end. I clutched on to it till my feet wrapped round the wooden post, and shinned down it to the coal pile, and turned.

The night was like day!

It was weirder than day.

All the plants in the garden were looking at me.

I went across the grass and over the chain link fence. I went up the slope to the cliff, and heard the sea. It took me five minutes, going fast, to reach it, and I stopped and gaped.

Below, everything was a lake of silver.

I could see one arm of the bay, a cold moon colour, and apart from that nothing but silver. The sea was breathing slightly, a soft shushing sound.

I went as close to the edge as I could, and looked over, and saw only the bulge of the cliff, and got on my stomach and leaned farther, and still saw it. The cliff bulged out so far, the sea at the base wasn't visible.

I remembered looking up the cliff and seeing the bulge on top. It was the right bit of cliff, anyway.

I looked round in the moonlight and wondered where to start. I thought I'd start on a few big outcrops of rock that stuck out of the tough, straggly grass. If the entrance to the path was so well concealed that no one had ever found it, it had to be an expert job.

I prowled round the shadowy parts with the flashlight.

I did it till the third heap of rock, when I twisted my ankle in a rabbit hole and came down hard. I rubbed the ankle and saw, in the flashlight, that it was twenty minutes to two. I thought that was enough. It was like looking for a needle in a haystack, and night was no time to do it. I'd do it by day, and it didn't matter if Annie was there or not. She didn't have to know what I was looking for.

I decided that and started getting up and saw it was a funny rabbit hole. It was a piece of slate. It had broken under my weight. I put the flashlight closer and saw the slate was the colour of the rock. It had been put there to look like rock. It would take a smart rabbit to do that.

I got on my knees and pulled the piece of slate out. It was a corner of a bigger piece, and I tried to pull that out, too. It was embedded in the tough grass roots and wouldn't come. But I broke some more and uncovered a black hole underneath. It didn't smell earthy or stale, the hole. A fine fresh breeze blew up it.

18

I sat back on my heels and blinked at it.

It still took a minute to realise I'd found the entrance.

THROUGH THE FACE

There were five steps, very steep, in something like a manhole. I went slowly down, shining the flashlight. The opening was narrow and irregular, but as I went lower it widened. At the bottom it was very wide. It was a room. It was square. It was cut in the rock.

I shone the flashlight round. The walls were regular, the roof and floor regular; all regular, and very neat, as if it had just been swept.

There was a hole in one wall, like a doorway. The breeze was coming through it. It was coming from a tunnel that I could see sloping sharply away. I bent and went in the tunnel and started shuffling cautiously down it. The breeze was stronger in the tunnel, and I could hear it. It had a husky sound like someone blowing a bottle. I could feel it plucking at my clothes.

I'd gone about twenty feet when I saw the gun. It was lying by a wall. I knew right away it was old. But when I bent and picked it up, I saw from the bugle-shaped end that it was hundreds of years old. It had lain here for centuries.

It gave me a strange feeling suddenly. It gave me a feeling I was in a tomb. I wondered if it was true ghosts came up and haunted places and put lights out. I thought I'd go now.

I was thinking that when the light went out.

I nearly fell down with fright.

I knew it couldn't be ghosts. There couldn't be any ghosts. It was just that the bulb had gone. It had to be.

In the pitch blackness I could hear my teeth rattling. I was in such a panic I couldn't tell if it was the breeze plucking at my clothes, or something else. I'd dropped the gun. I just hung on to the flashlight. I bent in a sort of crouch and gave it a threatening shake, and the batteries moved inside, and it came on again. The end had come loose.

I tightened the end and thought I'd definitely go now. I'd done enough for one night. It was two o'clock, an hour since I'd left home. I could get back here any time. I didn't have to do it all at once.

While I was thinking this, I was shuffling on. I thought I'd go a few paces more. Then a few more after that. I'd got over my panic. I thought while I was here I'd see what was at the end of the tunnel.

I got to a blank wall, and poked the flashlight round, and found the tunnel went in a sharp bend, and started round with it.

I went round, then round again, descending all the time, and was suddenly dazzled by a blinding mass of silver.

I'd come out to the cliff. I was below the bulge. The tunnel had cut right through it. I was perched on the west face with the wrinkled sea miles below.

There was a kind of zig-zag outside the tunnel, a slit in the rock. It zig-zagged down the cliff as far as I could see. It was the path.

Well, I'd found it. I could go now.

But I didn't go.

I had a crazy idea. I thought I'd see where the path went. I couldn't explain it. I just had to do it.

The path was in shadow, and I pointed the flashlight down and birds flew out. They flapped up one at a time like dusters. They did it slowly, as if they didn't want to do it at all. But they all did it, and in half a minute the zig-zag, right down to water level, was alive with gulls. The big silver birds wheeled in the night, not crying out, just flapping their wings. Right above the sea, I could see the step in the cliff sticking out.

It was so weird, it was like a dream.

The trench was cut deep in the cliff, about four feet. It was a long jagged tear, either a natural fault or deliberately cut.

Whether it was natural or not, someone had made steps in it. The first couple I could see quite clearly, although they were covered with crumbled rock from the cliff. The rest were so badly deteriorated there was just a bumpy downhill path. Storms, or birds, or the constant shower of debris from above had almost levelled out the steps.

I started slowly down them.

The surface was so crumbly, I couldn't step at all. I crammed the flashlight in my jeans, and went on my behind.

It took me half an hour, with rests in between.

On the last leg of the zig-zag the steps appeared

again as if the sea sometimes washed up. I got on my feet and walked to the bottom and hung on to the cliff there.

The sea was winking and slapping just below.

I can't explain now what I did.

I knew it would be a hard job scrambling back up the cliff. I knew it would take time.

I can't explain it. But in dreams you do things without explanation. And it's like a dream to me.

Even now, after everything—a fantastic dream.

I jumped, anyway.

WHO'S THERE?

I landed on the platform and flashed the light in the cave and saw it was deep (it is twenty-four feet). I examined it a long time before moving. I saw the floor was safe and inspected the roof and walls. I saw the iron bolts in the wall, and the barrel of hard tar secured there.

The floor was scattered with stones and rubbish flung in by the sea. It sloped down backwards, and there were two steps down to it from the platform. I went carefully down them and saw, in the floor of the cave, a hole. I shone the flashlight in it and saw water at the bottom and knew immediately it was the sea because it was moving. I also saw the rungs set in the side of the hole, and the chain secured to the third one.

I didn't look further round the cave.

I checked the chain.

I stood on the first rung and put weight on it, and it held, so I did the second and the third and grasped the chain and pulled. Something shifted at the other end, but it wouldn't come, and I put out my foot to go lower but found the next rung was in the water, so I went up and took my sneakers and socks off.

While I was at it, I took everything off. I took my windbreaker and pullover off, and my watch, then the rest, and wedged the flashlight near the hole, and just then the light shone back at me.

It wasn't my light. It came floating up out of the hole. It floated two or three feet and stopped, and my heart jumped in my throat.

I said, "Who's there?"

He said, "Who's there?"

A kid came out of the hole. He had nothing on.

I said, "How did you get there?"

He said, "How did you get there?"

He put out a hand and touched my forehead, so that a kind of headache came and went, very fast. He'd just been repeating what I said, but he said something else then. He said, "I came in my boat. It's here. You can see it."

He walked up the two steps to the platform and pointed and I followed him and saw it. It was a canoe, bobbing in the moonlight a few yards away. I hadn't seen a canoe as I came down the cliff. It was a funny time to be canoeing.

He said, "You're Barry, aren't you?"

I said, "Who are you?"

He said, "I'm Dido." (*Deedo*, he said it.)

I said, "How do you know my name?"

He said, "I've heard it."

"Are you on holiday here?" (He was fairer than the Seele kids. His hair was white.)

"Yes," he said. Come down the hole. There's a tunnel. I came through it. I've got a waterproof light. There's a barrel and a box there, both very old."

"Is it safe?" I said.

I said it for something to say. I had no idea of going down the hole with him.

"Sure. You push yourself under and walk. You just walk in the tunnel. When you need a breather, you come up this side. Or you go out in the sea. It's safe," he said.

He stepped down off the platform and walked to the hole.

"I'll go first," he said.

He went down the rungs and pushed himself under and the water turned bright green. After a while it faded, and the chain moved. It clanked up and down a few times as if he was tugging it. I didn't know if he was signalling me to follow. I didn't do anything. I just watched the hole, and in a few seconds it flashed green again, and he surfaced.

"You didn't come," he said.

I didn't know what to do. He'd seen I'd taken my clothes off as if I'd meant to try.

"Come," he said.

He backed away from the rungs, and I went down.

"Duck," he said.

I hung on to a rung and ducked, and came up panting. It was cold as ice.

"I'll go first," he said again. "Give me a tug when you want a breather."

He didn't look at me. He just ducked, and I took a breath and ducked, too.

It was emerald green in the tunnel.

His light was brighter in the water, and everything was magnified. I saw individual grains of sand floating. I saw my hands big and pink in front of me. I saw him big and pink. He was holding the light low and pointing it so that it lit up the place. We were walking in slow motion down a green crystal passage with an arched roof. He turned and saw my head slightly graze the roof, and he tapped his own and bent to show what I should do.

I nodded and he pointed to the chain. It was sagging along the slatey wall of the tunnel, rusted and flaking, and a few yards away two big objects, attached to it, moved gently up and down, partially blocking the tunnel.

I pulled myself along the walls, and got to the barrel and the box. They were painted with tar. He watched me feeling them, and motioned farther along. Then he looked at me and pointed upwards, to see if I needed a breather yet.

I shook my head, and he shone the light at the far end. Then he ducked under the obstruction, and I followed him.

It was only a few yards farther. A pulley was stuck in the wall and the chain ran through it. It was rusted and covered with barnacles. But I'd had enough suddenly. I needed air. I gave him a tug and pointed up, and turned. But he caught my arm and pointed the other way, towards the sea.

He didn't wait for my agreement. He just took off, with the light.

I followed close behind, my lungs bursting.

I saw him go out the end of the tunnel, and the light turned murkier.

He waited for me in the sea, keeping himself under.

He took my hand as I came out. I felt myself choking, and kicked out, and in seconds broke surface.

He backed off in the water as I gasped and coughed.

"We were down too long," he said. "I'm sorry."

"It's all right," I said.

"Come and rest on the boat."

It was bobbing a few yards away, and he swam to it. I waited awhile, coughing, before turning there, and he helped me in and I sat and got my breath. It was a little canoe, six or seven feet. All around the breeze was wrinkling the water.

He saw me rubbing myself in the breeze.

"Come and dry off," he said. "Over here."

He went to the end of the boat, and I followed. "There are two steps," he said, and watched while I went down. "Now in here," he said, and opened the door.

It was a room about thirty feet long. There was a carpet on the floor and a sofa all along one wall. There were easy chairs and a low table, and music was softly playing.

WHERE DO WE GO?

was dreaming. I knew it. It was three o'clock in the morning, and I was dreaming. My mother hadn't woken me to ask about the flashlight. I hadn't gone backwards out of the window, or down a cliff in the middle of the night. I hadn't swum to a canoe with a couple of steps (in a *canoe*?) down to a room thirty feet long. I'd dreamed it; was fast asleep now and dreaming in my bed.

"I have to wake up," I said.

"You're not asleep," he said.

He was smiling at me.

"Come and dry off."

He took my arm and led me through a doorway into a corridor, very long, with many rooms.

We were in a bathroom. The walls, the floor, the ceiling were of metal, but not of metal I'd ever seen. It shone softly, a bluish green. So did the sunken bath and the shower. We stood on a grid beside the shower and I felt immediately dry. The air didn't move. It was just dry; and so was I, in a second.

Minutes later we were dressed and I was seeing everything.

I won't put it now. For now I'll say I saw the sleeping quarters, the kitchen, the control room, and that later we drank tigra, and I felt marvellous. I felt wonderful. I knew I could jump any wall, or dive impossible distances. I could fly. (This is the tigra, and I'll tell more later.)

I also knew we'd taken off. There was no sensation of movement. I'd just felt it earlier, that dizzy fractional lurch.

Nothing of what was happening was believable to me. It just kept on happening, very fast. I had no time to believe or disbelieve. Yet I hadn't stopped thinking. I thought: he's from another world; but even as I thought it I knew it was mad. You couldn't come from other worlds. At school we'd heard why. The fastest thing in the universe was light. It was the same speed as radio waves. To send a signal to the moon took a second and a half. To the sun, it took six minutes. To the next star after the sun, four and a half years. Just to signal a planet where there might be life would take three hundred years; so how could there be flights of that distance, of that time?

I knew there couldn't be.

So I sat, not believing, not disbelieving, just nerving myself to ask the question. Finally, I blurted: "Where are you from?"

"From Egon," he said.

"Is that—another planet?"

"Not another planet."

"In outer space?"

"Not outer," he said.

"What do you mean?"

"Inner."

He laughed as my mouth dropped open, and

28

leaned over and patted me. He patted me like you pat a dog. "Inner space, Barry," he said. "There's a world below this world. There is a world under the sea. The real world. Egon. Look," he said.

We were in the main room, at the low table, and he slid a panel from beneath and studied it. Then he pressed something, and I felt the tremor again, but now like a high-speed elevator, slowing. He pressed once more and the room darkened and the wall lit up.

It took a moment to see that it wasn't the wall, but what was outside, that had lit up. The wall had become transparent; outside was the sea. It had lit up dimly, a dark soupy colour. I heard him muttering, and he did something else, and with a single giant flicker the whole sea lit up. It lit up for miles. It was the most fantastic thing I'd ever seen. It was not like sea. It wasn't even like water. There was no motion, no waves. It was clear as air, a pale honey colour. And everywhere there were mountains.

Before I could take it in, it all went out.

In the darkness I heard him muttering again. Then with a series of flickers, faster than sheet lightning, the whole world lit up; above, below, on all sides. We were poised in our chairs, and all the furniture poised with us; the entire structure of the boat transparent.

Miles above, through the ceiling, the sky flashed and glittered like a skin of mercury. Far below, there was a vast winding valley. It was mottled like a lizard, and on both sides of it foothills sloped. Immense terraced cliffs rose from the foothills, their castle-like tops facing each other. There were canyons between the cliffs, and swarming in and out of

them were millions of fish. There was an unbelievable multitude, of every colour. The walls and terraces were of every colour — purple, green,
tangerine. Ahead was a mountain range, and the
nearest peak was shining turquoise. There was a
forest on its crest.

My mouth was opening and closing, and I looked
at Dido and saw he'd not spared a glance for what
was outside. He was studying the panel. He said,
"Yes. There." And I looked where he pointed.

Beyond the turquoise mountain, far in the distance, soared three slender peaks. He pressed the
panel, and we moved. There was only the faintest
lurch, but now I saw how fast we moved. The cliffs
began hurtling past. The speckled valley below un-
ravelled like knitting wool. In seconds, the three
peaks were dead ahead, and he slowed the boat.

From a range of maybe ten miles, they stood
weirdly alone, towering pinnacles, rising abruptly
from the ocean bed like a cathedral.

"Now you'll see," Dido said, and we began to rise.
We rose gently, closing slightly with the pinnacles as
we went up the length of them. We rose a mile, two
miles, three; and all the time the pinnacles continued, straight up. Then the boat slowed to a stop, and
we broke surface into a fine summer's day.

Everywhere, the sun glinted. Where the pinnacles
had been, there was land. At this distance, four or
five miles, it was just a flat green smudge.

"I can't go closer," Dido said.

He twisted a control, and it *came* closer.

It did it in a series of jumps, as if the transparent
wall had become a lens. The green smudge enlarged
to a stretch of coast; then a beach; then a portion of

the beach. People were sunning and swimming from the beach. There were trees behind, and streets, and buildings. I could actually see a policeman directing traffic in a street; and behind him a building, and on the building a flag. It was a British flag.

"Where are we?" I said.

"Bermuda."

"But—we were in England. Only minutes ago!"

"That's not the point." He shook his head. "It's just a mountain top. Your whole world is mountain tops. You're mountain dwellers. Do you want to go to the other world, Barry? Below the abyss?"

The way he said it scared me, and I said nothing. He leaned across and touched my forehead. Again the swift headache came and went.

"You want to go to the other world, Barry," he said.

"Yes," I said.

"You want to go to Egon, below the abyss."

"Yes."

"Of course you do. I knew it," he said, and laughed, and we began the descent.

I know now that he did what he wanted with me. He put into my mind what he wanted me to know, and took out of it what he wanted me to forget.

I forgot my clothes, left in the cave, and the flashlight still switched on there. I forgot I had to get back, and all I had to get back to: my home, my parents, Sarah and Annie. I forgot all that. I forgot who I was.

Of the descent, all I know is that presently, cocking his head, he said, "Now. We're at it. The Glister Deep."

"What is it?"

31

"The way through the abyss. We're going in. You're too sleepy to see it, Barry."

"I'm not," I said. "I want to see it."

"You feel like a sleep."

"I don't. I don't want to sleep."

"You do," Dido said, and learned forward and touched me; and I passed into the other world, sleeping.

Under the Sea

THERE

don't know what to say about it.

I know I shouldn't put anything. I'll put it. I'll keep on putting it, just as it happened.

The first thing was a breeze, ruffling my hair, and his voice saying, "Wake up."

I stretched and stirred.

We were in a car, on a road, cruising.

Ahead, for mile upon mile, I could see the road twisting and looping.

It was an open car, and he was driving.

High above, the sun shone in a blue sky. To the right there were forest-clad hills, and to the left green meadows sloping to a river. There were cows at the water's edge, and across the river two people galloped on horseback.

He saw me rubbing my eyes and staring all about.

"Where are we?" I said.

"In Egon."

"Under the sea?"

"Miles under. Thirty miles at least, here."

He saw me peering up, and laughed.

"You won't see it," he said.

35

"But—how does it stay up?"

He laughed so much he had to slow the car.

"How does your sky stay up?" he said. "Or your sun? How does your ground stay down?" He wiped his streaming eyes. "Don't worry. I'll explain later. Though I don't know how much you'll understand," he added cheerfully.

He told me we were in tigra-nut country, and pointed out the details of the forest. And I looked at it, and at the meadows and the river, and blinked, but none of it changed. The sky was high and blue and the sun shone in it.

Sky and sun—below the sea?

"Don't worry," he said. "Breathe!"

I breathed. There was the most delicious scent in the air. I couldn't breathe in enough of it. It was coming from the forest, and I saw that the tigra trees were strange and beautiful, their trunks dappled with maroon and silver. From the high blue foliage large nuts drooped in clusters, like purple melons.

We were passing a small clearing in the forest, and I saw movement and wondered if it was animals.

"Not animals," he said. I hadn't said anything aloud. "They're tigra pickers."

And soon afterwards, at another clearing, I saw a group of them on the ground: men, stripped to the waist in the hot sun. There was something strange about them. I couldn't say what it was. They were clustered about a huge crate, like a boat, piled high with the purple nuts. Overhead a net was stretched between the trees and a chute led from it to the crate. Men were swaying overhead in the net and tumbling the great nuts down the chute. They waved, and Dido said, "We'll stop a moment."

There were thirty or forty men in the clearing, some working, others eating at a long table or lying in the sun. They recognised Dido, and called as we approached.

They stared curiously at me.

I'll say now how we were dressed.

We'd dressed in persongs on the boat. It's a one-piece tunic, the persong. It has a square neck or a round neck or even a high neck. (Girls wear a blouse below theirs with a kind of decoration or ornament at the throat.) Underneath there are short pants or long tights. The outfits are in varied colours, and in different patterns and materials.

Dido and I wore the same—they were his—so the men weren't staring at me for that. They were staring at my hair. Theirs was pure white, like his. But as hard as they stared at me, I stared harder. I saw what was so strange about them.

They were giants. They were several times the size of normal men. Their heads were enormous, and their hands, and everything about them.

They spoke to Dido, but they looked at me. Even the men working stopped and came to look at me. They were young, I could see, with sandals on their feet and cotton-like slacks half way to the ankle.

One of them bent and picked me up, like a puppy. In the hot sun a powerful odour came off him, not unpleasant, almost spicy. He held me with one hand and put the other under my chin and looked in my eyes. I felt again the sudden slight pain as when Dido had touched my forehead, and immediately he spoke English.

He said, "What's your name, big shot?"

I said, "Barry."

"Where do you come from, Barry?"

"England."

"What happens in England?"

His eyes were green and huge. It was like talking to a monument. I could feel his breath like a breeze, and his deep voice rumbling through my body.

I said, "I'm at school there."

"Are you? And how old are you?"

"Twelve."

He almost dropped me. He laughed so much I shook all over. He repeated what I had said to the others, and one of them took me from him and had a look at me. They were passing me from hand to hand when Dido stopped them.

"We can't stay here," he said to me, agitated. "My father knows I'm here. He doesn't know about you. I shouldn't have done it. Come. And don't ask questions about the car," he said. We were walking to it, and he saw I was just going to start asking. For one thing, there were no wheels on it.

We got in and I watched what he did. He pressed a couple of buttons and it rose slightly and took off. It took off silently with just the sound of the breeze, so I knew it wasn't a hovercraft or a jet. I couldn't tell what sort of craft it was.

"What was so funny about my age?" I said.

"They thought you'd be my age."

"What's your age?"

"Ninety-nine," he said.

He saw my mouth drop open.

"My little sister is sixty," he said. "Our baby, who sleeps all day, is eighteen."

"Eighteen *years*?"

"Years. . . . You won't understand. And I

38

shouldn't have got you. Maybe my father does know." He was frowning, rubbing his face. "And I have an important exam coming up. You're going to be nothing but trouble."

"Well, what do you—"

"Just shut up," he said.

"Look, I didn't ask you to—"

"Good night," he said, and touched my forehead, and I was asleep again.

The sun was lower when I woke.

We were in the air. We were coming in to land.

"There's an inn here," he said, "and friends of mine. There's no projector. My father can't come in here."

I couldn't make anything of this, but he was nodding and seemed cheerful now. He patted me on the head, and I looked carefully at him. Ninety-nine!

"It's crude, this place," he said, "but it will do. Mura was my nurse. She'll help. She'll have to. I want to keep you for a bit. Afterwards, well. . . . She'll keep quiet. I'll make her."

I didn't like the sound of any of this. I didn't like the "afterwards." I didn't like him putting me off to sleep whenever he felt like it, or patting me on the head like a pet.

We were driving along a country lane, and I watched him nodding his head and sucking his teeth, and I looked up and thought of the sea pounding on top of the sky.

I thought of waking in the world below it; of the giants in the tigra forest, the little sister of sixty, the eighteen-year-old baby who slept all day; also of the car that could turn into a plane. At this time I'd forgotten the boat, and the canoe, and everything before it. I knew only what he wanted me to know, and I didn't know if it was a dream or a nightmare.

THROUGH THE PROJECTOR

There was a wooden hall in the inn, with a reception counter and chairs and tables—enormous, all of them. The moment we walked in he began impatiently calling, "Mura! *Mura!*" and a woman came hurrying in.

She was a giantess, bigger even than the men in the forest, and fatter, and she roared with delight at the sight of him.

"Dido!" she cried, and bent and picked him up and hugged him. But he kicked and struggled so much in the air—he was fifteen feet in the air—that she put him down, and he began shouting at her.

She roared pleadingly back. Then his eyes went to a large metal frame, like a doorway, set in the wall opposite the counter.

"They've got a projector!" he yelled. "My father's been in."

He began shouting again, trying to restrain her as she moved behind the counter. But she fiddled with something, and the frame lit up. It glowed a moment,

40

and the area in front of it glowed. A woman was there. She wasn't on a screen. She was there. She was sitting at a table with flowers. We were standing right in front of her.

The woman spoke to him, but her eyes remained on me, and presently he pushed us both forward into the glow, and we were there with her in the room. I looked all round the room. I looked behind me, and the room still continued. I wasn't in the inn any more. I was in this other room. It was the strangest room. It was made of mother-of-pearl or shell. It was in the air. There was a long curving window, and through it I saw sky. The whole room was flickering in the sky.

I felt dizzy and faint, with a pain in my head, and I turned and found the woman looking at me.

"Barry," she said.

"Yes," I said.

"I am Dido's mother. Do you understand?"

"Yes."

"Do you know where you are?"

"No," I said. It seemed safest to say it. I had no idea, anyway. I didn't even know where I was *supposed* to be now.

She gave me a long look.

Dido began to speak but she cut him off with a few sharp words, and suddenly she wasn't there, and the whole room had vanished. We were back in the inn, and he nearly went mad.

"We've got to stay here!" he shouted. "They won't let me keep you. You've got to be erased here?"

"Erased?"

"My father will be coming through. They'll do it here."

41

"What do you mean, erased?" I said.

"*Erased.* Can't you understand anything? You've *got* to be erased. But I wanted to keep you for a bit. I wanted to take you to Mount Julas, and Plum Lake, and the power slopes, and sky-diving. And to feed you ragusas, and stardew, and pansa patty. And to see them go crazy when I took you to parties. They'd never have dared get you themselves. Then they could have erased you."

"Dido," I said. I was so confused I could hardly think. "About getting erased—"

"Just shut up," he said.

"But—"

"I'm going to my room—if this fool has kept it for me. And you can't be left on your own. Come," he said, and grabbed my arm and walked me through the hall.

We went into a room—a huge one like a ballroom, with a bed in it—but he didn't give it a glance. He just pressed a button in the wall and the opposite wall turned to glass and opened, and he strode out to a verandah. It was a long wooden verandah. A giant was leaning his elbows on a barred wooden railing on it, but he went as we came out. Dido climbed the bars of the railing and leaned over the top, and so did I. All round was beautiful country, with forested hills swooping to a curving river, and hazy mountains in the distance.

I couldn't take in anything of what was happening to me. I hadn't for hours. I just said the first thing that came in my head.

I said, "Dido, when you erase a person—"

"You take their memory away," he said abruptly.

42

"You erase the knowledge from their minds, like when you're born or when you die."

"Does it hurt?"

"You'd be asleep."

"Then what would happen?"

"You'd be back in the cave."

"What cave?" I said.

He looked at me. Then he smiled. "Well, I did it," he said. "I erased you. And I haven't even studied it yet. Putting your memory back isn't the same as erasing it," he said. "But let's try."

We got down from the railing and he began feeling my head. He lifted my face so that I looked into his green eyes.

Exactly when it happened, I saw he knew it had happened.

"You can remember the cave," he said.

"Yes."

"And the cliff. And going out the window."

"Yes." I wondered how he knew I'd gone out the window.

"And the storm the day before—when I saved you."

"When *you* saved me?"

"You were drowning. I watched you. I watched you for a couple of days, on and off."

I remembered the feeling of being watched.

Just then I remembered something else.

"Did you *make* me come down that cliff?" I said.

"I put it in your mind. I'm not good at it yet." He was looking at me seriously. "Anyway, you'll go back and forget now. You'll forget all this. And I wanted to show you so much."

43

I couldn't believe what I'd seen already. Had I really been in a canoe that had turned into a submarine; seen mountains in the sea; visited Bermuda within minutes?

"I'm dreaming," I said. "I know it. I'm not under any sea."

"You are," he said.

"With another sun, and a sky, and forests—"

"Look, you're not going to remember any of it," he said, "not after they've properly erased you. So there's no harm in telling you now."

And that's what he did, on the verandah and in the room, while we waited for the people to come and erase me; and I began to learn the things that I should not have learned.

THE STONE BRAIN

He said we were made of the sea. He said almost three-quarters of our bodies was liquid, and that our blood and our sweat and our tears were salty because the sea was salty.

He said everything came from the sea; everything had started there, and life on the globe was in just a thin skin round the edge, like the skin of an apple.

He said that the skin was in three layers, and the exposed outer one, where the mountains jutted out of the sea, was the world of the "mountain dwellers." At its highest point it was only five and a half miles high (this was Mount Everest), and even that was too high for any life. There was little life above four miles. Jet planes rarely flew higher than six. So this was the narrowest and meanest layer.

Below it was the sea, and this was seven miles deep, with mountains higher than Everest, and life in every part of it. He said creatures on other planets thought earth was mainly water, with the life on it mainly water-life; and this was true because water covered two-thirds of it.

Not only that: there *was* more of everything under water. There were more creatures and vegetable life. There were more minerals and chemicals, more oil, coal, gold, food—everything; which made sense because things didn't just start in the sea but also ended there.

He said that dozens of times mountain ranges had built up from the sea, and life and civilisations had formed on them; and dozens of times they'd worn down again and returned to the sea as dust. And over millions of years, the dust and sediment had formed into "sedimentary" rock and pushed up into mountains, and the whole process had restarted. He said that in the last 500 million years alone, this had happened half a dozen times; although by then the people had gone to Egon.

I'm trying to keep it simple.

It wasn't simple when he said it.

It's only a fraction of what he said.

Most of what he said I couldn't understand. There

45

weren't any words to make me understand. He said my brain wasn't big enough, and it never would be. He said it was like trying to tell a dog. He said he'd done all this stuff himself when he was sixty, years before, when his brain was ready. He said his sister hadn't started yet because hers wasn't ready. All their eighteen-year-old baby could do, so far, was play the violin.

I know it looks mad.

I thought I was mad.

I found I wasn't later; but I can't stop now. I've got to keep going.

He said that the land above the sea used to be one continent. There was no Asia, Europe, Africa, America, Australia. They were joined. And the climate was good and everything grew bigger in it. There weren't grotesque things like huge flying beasts. They came later, with even weirder creatures, after the mess-up. Thousands of different forms came later, and then passed out of existence.

At this earlier time, with conditions stable for millions of years, all life on the continent developed fully. There were more apes and man-like creatures. But man was the most intelligent. There were no black men or yellow men or white men; all were brown and of the same build and appearance; and they controlled the life on the planet.

At this time nuclear energy (he only mentioned it because I asked him) was already buried far into the past. It was as ancient as the discovery of fire. He said that for ages there'd been flights to the stars. And I've got to interrupt again, because of what I put earlier about the impossibility of reaching the stars and how the speed of light was the fastest thing in the universe and it would take too long.

He just looked at me when I said that. He didn't know how to explain it to me. He said could I remember what my bedroom looked like at home? I said I could. He said could I remember where I put my watch in the cave? I said I could. He said in that case a part of me had already moved faster than the speed of light. He said it was a question of using that part. He said the first twenty-five years at school were spent just learning the idea of it. It was as basic as reading and writing. It was as basic as the difference between brain and mind.

I said what was the difference between brain and mind, and again he looked at me and hardly knew what to say. He said it was obvious what the difference was. He said you got people with identical brains but you couldn't get them with identical minds. Making a brain work was what produced mind. Brain was a basic thing like stone.

I don't want to go on, but ideas keep coming back. He said if you blew up a balloon, and drew a map of the world on it, and let the balloon down, you'd see not only that all the continents come together more or less as they used to be, but that what they used to be was the shape of a brain.

He said so many things.

He gave me the look you give a dog when it can't understand. He said we'd skip it and he'd tell me about Egon.

He said millions of years ago science had become so advanced that they needed a better power source than the sun. The sun was too tiny a star for the power they needed. In exploring the universe they'd found many stars more useful than the sun.

The idea was to pick one with a suitable planet and move there. But the problem was to find a planet as suitable as earth. Earth was the finest and most beautiful planet anywhere. So a different idea had developed.

Instead of finding another planet, they decided to shift the earth. They'd focus all they could of the sun's energy and use it to launch earth into a different star system. There were disputes about it for generations, and it was difficult (it meant making changes to replace the gap left by earth in the solar system), but it was possible, so they tried it.

They tried it, and failed; and that was the mess-up, he said.

He said it started with a gigantic lurch which shifted the equator and made it into the north and south poles. It split up the whole continent of land. And it split up the foundation underneath.

He said the foundation was the third layer of the earth's skin, the crust. He said that this layer was thicker than the other two layers put together. It was thirty miles deep. It supported everything on top, the sea and the land.

When it split, it split into six main "plates." One carried away North and South America. Another carried most of Asia, Europe, and part of the Atlantic. Another carried the whole Pacific Ocean, and so on.

And a crazy cycle of weather changes began: ice ages, tropical ages, then ice ages again—as if the great stone brain had gone mad when it split. But before then they'd taken everything they needed from on top and gone down to Egon. Egon had been discovered long before, and he was just telling me how when Mura began roaring and said his father was in the projector.

We were in the room by that time, and she switched the projector on there, too. A girl came through it and told him to wait. Then she looked round the room and went.

Dido licked his lips nervously.

He said, "Barry, I'd better say goodbye now. He might erase you himself. He can come in and do that. He can do everything like that."

"But—"

"Don't say a thing. It's just that I wanted to show you everything. Egonia, the fantastic city, and Mount Julas, and Plum Lake. . . . Well—goodbye."

He was patting my head, and I didn't know whether to pat his. I didn't know how you said goodbye here. I just said awkwardly, "Goodbye," when the projector glowed again, and a man was there. He was speaking to someone beyond us, and the girl we'd seen was putting papers on his desk. He was a stern-faced man. He didn't bother coming into the room. He just stayed where he was and looked straight at us.

I felt Dido almost shrivel beside me, and he tried to say something. But the man cut him off, and spoke a few sentences more. Then his face seemed to soften, and I looked at Dido's and saw a look of surprise and delight come over it. He began speaking, but the man just gave him a nod and the projector went dead.

"Oh, boy!" Dido cried. "Oh, Egon!"

"What is it?"

"There's a storm up there. They've made inquiries. Nobody can get to that cave. They won't be able to get to it for three days. You can stay! You can come home with me!" He was pulling my ears and patting my head.

And that's how it happened. It's how I came to see it. It's how I remember what I'm not supposed to remember.

THE FABULOUS CITY

I remember another road, and doing 300 miles an hour on it. And he must have told me how transport worked by then because I wasn't surprised when we flew.

It worked by magnetism. It used the earth as a magnet which could attract or repel like any other magnet. By using the controls you could go forward or backward, up or down, and by using the power you could increase or decrease speed.

We came to traffic, and he muttered and slowed. He said there was a speed limit—and not because of the danger of crashes, since vehicles couldn't crash. When you switched on, you also switched on your "force line," which meant that cars repelled each other and couldn't touch, however fast they were going. But they repelled each other so violently at speed that equipment and people could be damaged. And you had to be careful about spare parts.

(The spare parts weren't only for machines. But I'll come to that. There's no pain in Egon.)

We had to slow so much that he looked anxiously at the sky, and I saw the sun was setting. Clouds had appeared, and the countryside was turning mauve.

"I'll have to turn off," he said, and began muttering again. And after a few minutes we did turn off, up a country lane.

We went a few miles, and he stopped and switched on a panel on the dashboard. It lit up a bluish colour, with little points of light moving in every direction on it. Then he pressed something else, and we took off. We took off vertically. The ground seemed to telescope below, and I could see the highway, and on all sides rolling countryside. Then he stopped, and we hovered while he studied the panel.

"I'm not supposed to do it," he said, and muttered a bit, and began flying forward, very fast. We did it for just a few minutes, Dido studying the panel all the time. Then he said, "Now—right ahead!" and I looked and saw . . . something like sprinkles on a cake. It was a little mass of little dots of colour.

"I can't go closer," he said, and stopped, and we stayed still in the air.

He moved a control on the dashboard and, as before, the glass of the windscreen became a lens, and the little dots moved forward.

In short, sharp movements the dots turned into shapes—into cubes, spirals, octagons, needles; all marvellously coloured, and sparkling so brilliantly in the last of the light that I gasped out loud.

I didn't know where to look first. The shapes moved closer and closer. The whole screen filled up with them.

They were buildings—I could see now. And the teeming mass of them was a city. But it was like a carnival. Some of the buildings were like twists of striped candy; others like flowers or mushrooms. One had a pear-shaped dome, the colour of a pearl.

He heard me exclaiming, and laughed himself.

"You had to see it in the light," he said. "It will be dark when we get there."

"It's beautiful!" I gasped.

"The *most* beautiful," he said. "It's the finest city on the earth—the finest there's ever been. I'll show you the centre, the old part."

He touched a control, and the city began rushing past in a great blaze of colour, the fantastic buildings whirling away on every side. Then he slowed and several beautiful plazas came into view. Broad avenues radiated into the most spacious of the plazas. There were fountains spaced out over it, and in the centre was a tree.

It was the strangest tree.

It was huge, a luminous purple, and its upper branches were in constant motion. There was water all around it. Fish were in the water; they were going in a steady procession round the tree, and I caught the flash of tails in the last sunlight.

"What is it?" I said.

"The president's palace."

"The tree is?"

"It's the symbol of Egon. It's the image of a sea anemone. A sea anemone is an animal but it acts like a plant. It can move if it wants to, but it doesn't. It stays in one place and gets everything it needs with its tentacles. It's the sign that we'll never try and move again. . . . Well, you've seen it. And we'd better go!" he said urgently. "We've been spotted."

Among the little lights on the panel, one had begun to flash red and was growing bigger.

He touched the controls and we dropped sharply.

The moon came out, and the stars.

I watched them.

Moon and stars—under sea, under earth?

He wouldn't answer my questions. He just concentrated on his driving. There were several lanes of traffic now.

Lighted restaurants passed, floating in the air; people danced in them, in the air. I watched them bobbing over the countryside. But now I could see the glow of Egonia; a vast cloud of purple and gold in the sky. I couldn't take my eyes off it. Yet when we came to the city, I couldn't all at once understand it. There was no ordinary light, but everything glowed. The roads glowed, from within, a pale golden colour. The buildings glowed, in every colour. We passed one of the multicoloured spirals I'd seen in the sunset. Its twisting candy stripes, of green and pink and white, were glowing the same colours, though more softly, and sparkling all the way up with pinpoints of light that were evidently windows.

On every side the fabulous structures passed, and as we crossed an intersection I could see along the broad thoroughfares hundreds more of them. The pavements were thronged with people, the night air full of the buzz of conversation and laughter and music. Shops and stores of all kinds were open, and people were seated at outdoor cafes. As before, it looked like a huge carnival, but now that I was in it, even better. There was an air of such excitement and gaiety everywhere that I found myself laughing out loud. And it didn't seem strange because most other people were, too. When I looked at Dido he was grinning away himself.

"What do you think of it?" he said.

"It's the most fantastic town I ever saw!"

"It's the most fantastic anyone ever saw. It has the best of all towns in it. You can do anything with a town. It doesn't have to be just streets with big buildings," he said. "If a building gets boring, you put another one up. Most of these have only been up a few hundred years."

Just then we passed one like a pineapple, an elongated pineapple, and I could see people sitting out on the glowing segments.

We were going slowly now in the traffic, and he was careless with his driving. Sometimes he didn't slow in time when the car in front slowed, and I felt the rebound as the force line stopped us from touching, and the car behind rebounded from us.

(And there's so much I've no time to put. I haven't mentioned the "rainbows," where the cars from the intersections passed over; or how the giants everywhere so soon became normal to me.)

We just drove on. We drove a long time through the fabulous city before I began to recognise again the areas I'd seen from the air. I saw the series of beautiful plazas begin, and the broad ceremonial avenues, and then the broadest avenue of all, with the sea anemone palace at the end. There was a huge glow of purple in the sky; and I could see the town going on beyond it.

"Are we going to the other side of town?" I said.

"We're going *into* town," he said. "The centre." And just then we swung round a huge square, and came to golden gates, and uniformed giants at each side saluted and opened the gates. We drove through, and I looked at Dido, but he didn't look back.

Fountains were playing all over the plaza, but the splashing sound didn't come from them. It came from the immense moat all round the palace. Spouts of water and spray were flung high as the procession of fish cruised steadily round, and I saw with incredulity that they were whales.

We took a rainbow over the whales, and headed for the palace, and I said, "Dido."

"I know," he said. "I'm sorry. I should have told you. My father's president of Egon. He runs the world. Welcome to the palace."

THE ANEMONE
PALACE

It's no use saying each new thing I saw
was more fantastic than the last. It's true, but what's
the use? The palace at Egonia is so fantastic there
are no words for it. Dido told me the style had
always been the same but every few thousand years
they rebuilt it, and this one was due for rebuilding
now because it was nine thousand years old. All the
materials of the world were in it. There were rooms
built of diamond, and of ruby.

Also, it was enormous. The whales looked ordinary because it was so enormous. It had a "stalk"
over a hundred yards across, and I don't know how
high (except it was over half a mile), and the rooms
were in the stalk.

The entrance was bustling with officials, and we
went through the main hall to the elevators and
escalators that circled the building. The private
apartments were on the top floor, and he took me up
in the elevator right away.

It's all a jumble to me what happened after we got
out of that elevator. A little kid was waiting for us
there (this was his sister, the sixty-year-old, Neila),

and she couldn't stop looking at me and touching me and feeling my hair. She kept dancing up and down tugging me, and he muttered that we had to go to the nursery because she wanted to show me to the baby.

We went into the nursery and there was the baby, sitting up in its cot, playing the violin.

It was amazing. It was playing the violin really well, and the giant nurse was sitting there singing away and nodding in time.

The moment it saw me it gave a yell and threw the violin away (there were smashed-up violins all over the room) and started reaching out to me, bouncing up and down in the cot. Everyone was grinning at the baby, so I grinned too, though is scared the life out of me. It had a big head. It had big green eyes. They all had green eyes and white hair, and the baby saw I was different.

The nurse picked the baby out of the cot, and while it was pulling at my hair, Dido's mother came in. I recognised her right away, from the projector, but she just nodded coldly at me.

Then we were in another room, the living room, just the three of us; and I saw she was furious.

She was like a queen, Dido's mother. She wore jewels in her hair, and had it piled high on her head, which made her taller. She was colossal, anyway; like a huge painted statue twenty feet tall. She barely looked at me, and I was too frightened to look up at her.

I looked round the room instead.

I knew I'd seen it before; that I'd even been in it before. I'd been in it through the projector. And I realised now what was so weird about it.

It was a sea shell.

It was a gigantic, perfect, beautiful sea shell, with a soft pink glow.

It had a long curved window, the mouth of the shell, that looked out high over the city. Through the shell of the ceiling, you could see the tentacles flickering above.

Dido spoke English so I'd understand, and she answered him the same way. She said his father was so angry with him he'd be lucky to keep his vehicle. She said, for a start, there was no way he'd be going to Plum Lake.

He nearly went out of his mind.

He said he *had* to go. He said all his group was going, and he was booked in for a week, and he was going to take me.

She told him not to shout. She said he should have thought of Plum Lake before bringing me. She said in any case he couldn't go now; and he had social duties tonight, so he'd better get himself properly dressed. Then she dismissed him, and we went to his room.

It was all of tigra wood, his room. It was maroon and silver, and full of the fascinating smell of tigra, so that I couldn't breathe in enough of it.

But he was gloomy, kicking things about.

"Never mind," he said at last, and patted my head. "We'll have a good time tonight, anyway."

He said his "social duties" were a round of student parties he had to attend. He had to make a speech at each about the coming exams. They were important exams, to be held after the holidays, and the results would decide what each of them would study next year, when they'd be a hundred, and for the following eighty years till they started university.

I couldn't cope with any of this. I just couldn't handle it. I said did he really mean *years*?

He said he did. He said the difference between us was the difference between people and dogs in the world above. He said people above lived seven times longer than dogs. But people in Egon lived over seven times longer than *people* above. He said they lived to seven or eight hundred. They developed more slowly. There was more of them to develop. They had igger brains. He said their baby already had a brain bigger than any professor's above. But they wouldn't start training its brain for another thirty years yet, because it still had a lot of developing to do.

He told me more about brains and how you trained them, but he did it while we were in the shower, and the shower was so fantastic, I hardly heard him.

It was there in the room. It was a grill in the floor, six feet square. You stood on the grill, and jets rose and lifted you. You could lie or roll or sit in the air, as you wanted. The water was slippery at first and you "soaped" with it; then it changed to ordinary water, and you sluiced off.

The shower went on for a few minutes and then lowered you to the grill and switched off; and if you wanted another you pressed on the grill and it started again. It was so great I *had* another. But he yelled at me to hurry; so I stood on the drying grill for a second, and joined him.

He'd yelled from another room; his walk-in wardrobe. He had fifty or sixty persongs in there, on hangers. He had racks of tights and shoes. He said in the evening you wore tights and shoes. He chose a silver persong for himself with green tights, and a yellow one for me with blue tights; and shoes with silver buckles for us both.

I thought I looked crazy. But the whole evening was crazy. It was the first time I went out in Egon. It was the first time I saw how they lived, or tasted their food. It was the first time I hit anyone of ninety-nine.

I WALK ROUND ME

I was dazed the whole of that night. Wherever I went I was pinching myself to be sure I wasn't fast asleep and dreaming. They were treating me like a trained monkey. I had to punch a kid's nose for him.

The kid was astonished. They were all astonished. His nose bled, and he dabbed it, and looked at the blood, and couldn't think why I'd done it.

(They don't fight in Egon. Because they have no pain, they can't hurt each other.)

He saw I was angry, and he saw the blood coming from his nose, but he couldn't connect the two. It made as much sense to him as if I'd gone and hit the wall.

But I was angry before then.

The parties were all for students of Dido's group, and he was chuckling as we drove to the first. He said we'd give them a surprise.

We got to the first, and he told the giant at the door not to announce us, and we went into the hall, and heard where the party was, and sneaked in.

There were twenty or thirty kids in the room, but half a dozen in the centre were causing most of the noise, and the rest were laughing at them.

Nobody noticed us at first. Then Dido gave a cough, and a girl who was drinking tigra looked round and saw him. Then she saw me, and dropped the tigra. She dropped it on a kid who was sitting on the floor, and the tigra went frothing and curling all over him, and everyone looked round.

Dido broke out laughing at their expressions. Then the kids in the middle of the room vanished, and everyone almost collapsed at *my* expression.

I was looking for the ones who'd vanished.

"Which ones?" Dido said.

"There were five or six of them. They were here," I said. I walked to where they'd been.

"Here?" he said.

"Right here. Didn't you see them?"

He winked and stepped aside, and I was standing next to myself. I was standing right beside myself. "There were five or six of them. They were here," I said. (At least, the other kid, who was me, said it.)

"Here?" Dido's voice said.

"Right here. Didn't you see them?" this other me said, and suddenly froze there with his mouth open, and I realised it was a full-size image of me, and that someone had recorded it; also that the kids I'd seen before had been in a recording. The other me was still standing there. I walked all round him. I saw a back view of me. I put out a hand and it went right through me. Then the other me vanished, and I was left there with my hand in the air, looking a fool, and everyone was curled up laughing. So I laughed, too. But it started then. I had an idea I'd be punching someone's nose.

Also they started touching my head, so that I had a series of the stinging headaches. And after it, they spoke English. Some did it better than others; and Dido did it best of all. He had, right from the start.

Then they were all round me, asking questions, and this kid asked if I'd ever had a tail, and I punched his nose for him.

He didn't make a row. Nobody made a row, and I said I was sorry, and he said he was.

I was just dazed. I was confused the whole night. There was so much going on. They could do everything. They could play any musical instrument. There was a game where they had to give clues in pictures, and they painted the pictures. They painted quickly and fabulously. They could do all kinds of tricks, like hopping on one hand. They could do anything any Olympic champion could do, or any musician or any artist or dancer. I felt like an animal. I felt dumb and stupid with them.

And there was the food and drink. They were drinking tigra everywhere, and I didn't explain it before.

It's silver. It's pure silver, with maroon stripes inside like raspberry ripple, except they move the whole time inside the silver. The drink swirls in the glass, and it swirls in your mouth, and it tastes like a tigra forest smells. It's delicate, silvery, but better than that. You can't stop drinking it. It coats your stomach silver, and acts on your brain. It makes you want to do things.

And stardew; fantastic stardew!

It's so powerful, nobody knew its effect on me. It comes from a mountain flower. The flower is deep violet, with a white centre, the cup. During the night a drop of "dew" comes up from the plant into the cup. It evaporates after dawn so they have to get it before then. They freeze it right away and mix it with petals into a violet gum. It takes hundreds of flowers to make a portion of gum. You have it ice cold, wrapped in stardew leaves. It's so cold you can hardly taste it.

They were all watching me while I tasted it. I unwrapped the leaves and licked the gum, and couldn't taste anything, so I licked it again. I still couldn't taste anything but the roof of my mouth seemed to rise suddenly. It seemed to rise into a huge vaulted arch like a cathedral. It was a cathedral full of violets. I was walking down long corridors with soaring stone pillars, breathing and drinking violets. An organ was playing violet music.

I was aware they'd sat me down, and that I was swaying dizzily. I could see their grinning faces outlined in violet. They were feeling my head and getting all my sensations.

They chewed up their own gum, and I don't know who had mine. I didn't try any more. They thought it might blow my brain. And that's how it went on.

I don't know how many parties we went to. I know the main topic at all of them was Plum Lake. Wherever we went they talked about it. They said it was the most terrific fun you could have anywhere.

63

And I know I was a sensation everywhere; that they couldn't stop looking at me and touching me and asking questions. But it's gone from me now. It's all just a mix-up now.

Dido made a speech wherever we went, and then we were back at the palace. I remember him telling me about places he was going to take me to instead of Plum Lake. He was going to take me to a famous river with a famous waterfall.

They'd put an extra bed for me in his room, and I must have been in it when his father came. I don't remember that properly, either. (Perhaps he erased the visit. Perhaps Dido just told me about it.)

But he came. And what he said changed the plans about the famous river and the waterfall. He said he'd thought again and made arrangements, and Dido could take me to Plum Lake; except instead of having a whole week for himself he could have just two days with me. In two days I had to be out of Egon.

The only thing I remember is Dido talking about it. He talked for hours. But he could only use words that were in my head, and I didn't have many for the kind of things at Plum Lake.

As for what was under it, he said nothing. He knew I had no words at all for that. And where am I to find them now? I'd died by then. I died there.

Under Plum Lake

THE LAKE

It's twelve miles long and three miles wide, and it's the finest place on earth. This is what they say, and they know all the places on earth.

It's shaped like a plum, and surrounded by rugusa plum trees. The roots of the trees are in the water, and the water is the same colour as the plums—a deep purple blue.

It's just wonderful. It's marvellous.

It's the only place ragusas grow. It's the only place you can get them. They don't keep. They only last an hour after they're picked. They send them round twice a day to all the hotels and guest houses; they send the exact number, one for each person booked in.

You see the lake first from two miles up. You turn a corner on the mountain road, and there it is, deep in the cleft of the valley. It's very warm there.

All down the valley, rooftops peep out of the trees, and at the bottom is the brilliant purple blue of the lake. But what I saw first were the kites. The air over the lake was full of kites. Then I saw there were people in the kites.

All of the drive so far had been fantastic. We'd gone through mountains. Now for the last couple of miles we went slowly. The road was like a corkscrew and people were strolling down it. I saw the gardens of the hotels on all sides. I saw the children's hotels, with the hammocks. I saw the pleasure dromes.

We drove to the far side of the lake, to a children's hotel that was almost on the water. The hammocks were slung between trees all over the garden.

We booked in and he signed for things: power slopes, skydiving, jubal-racing. I'll do all that. I'll do it later. Right now I'll do the place.

The first thing is the air. The air is different everywhere in Egon. It smells different in different places. Here, it's from the ragusas. The trees give off a gas. It's a kind of laughing gas. You go about as if you're walking on air. (When you leave a pleasure drome, you *are* walking on air: your feet are just off the ground.)

The trees get the gas from the water, and the water gets it from the springs in the lake. The water is unbelievable. You wash in it. You drink it. It tastes of flowers; it tastes of grapes.

The place holds 200,000 people, and there are over a thousand hotels and guest houses, but you rarely see them. They're tucked into gardens.

People get just ten weeks here during their whole life. They don't have to take a week at a time. They can take two days or three. They say a week here is like three months anywhere else. The reason is, you don't sleep. You take five-minute naps between activities. A nap is like a whole night's sleep, though old people sleep longer.

(It took me some time to spot old people. They're

68

over seven hundred years old, but they don't look it. They don't move slowly, or get ill. They can do anything anyone else can. They just have no eyebrows and their hair is thinner; it's the only way you can tell them.)

All round the lake is a promenade, nearly thirty miles long, with various pleasure gardens; and there are quays and jetties jutting out into the lake. You can eat where you want. You can do almost anything you want. Everything is free.

The one thing you've got to do is be on the ground at ragusa time. You can miss it if you want, but you'd be crazy. It takes up to an hour to eat a ragusa. The fastest you could do it is twenty minutes, but there's no sense in eating it fast. The slower you eat, the more you have.

It was after eleven when we booked in, so we got our ragusas right away. Just while we were booking in, twenty or thirty kids turned up for theirs, and I saw some from the night before. They yelled with surprise to see us, and we all went out and ate ragusas in our hammocks.

A ragusa is a giant plum, eight inches long. You hold it by a stalk at one end and peel off the point at the other. You peel it like a banana. Inside, the fruit is crisp like a pineapple, but chewy. It's as chewy as toffee. As you chew it, the part you've eaten grows back in place. It's the gas inside. It keeps replacing what you've eaten. It does it for sixty minutes, and then the gas goes and it melts.

It's juicy and sweet like a plum, except no one would come down from sky-diving just for a plum.

It's the laughing gas. It's the floating feeling.

You swing in your hammock, and watch the

ragusa grow, and you can't stop laughing. You tell jokes.

We did that, and later we ate.

Then we went up to the power slopes.

He hadn't told me it was the most dangerous sport in the world. He hadn't told me the things that could go wrong. I was just scared out of my life. I was so scared I knew I couldn't bear it.

THE POWER SLOPES

You wear ski clothes up there. You wear snow goggles. It's the top of Mount Julas, and the light is blinding. We went up on the fast cable, and he gave me a ski practice. They have a practice slope for beginners.

I'd never done any skiing. He put my skis on and attached the sticks; and I fell over right away. It's power skiing.

The controls are in the sticks. There's a switch in each handle, with three positions.

With the switch up, the power is off, which means you ski normally, on the ground.

In the middle position, power is on the skis, and they lift off the ground. They lift about four inches off.

In the bottom position power is in your suit as well as your skis, which means you can't touch ground, either.

It's very tricky. You can't hit ground, but you can overbalance and go tumbling in the air with your skis flying.

He gave me a practice with everything switched on, so I could get my balance. I toppled a few times, but I got it.

Then we did a few with just the skis switched on. It's dangerous, because you can go downhill fast—faster than on snow—so if you fall you're dragged fast. I didn't manage that so well.

With everything switched off, I couldn't manage at all. I just went sliding and falling.

He got impatient and said we'd skip it, because he had to do a run. He said, "We'll do one together later. I'll help you. You can watch for now."

We went to the starting point, and when I saw the run I nearly fainted.

A girl was just doing it.

I saw her flying through the air.

The run is seven miles long. It starts at Mount Julas, goes steeply downhill for a mile, then you fly over a dip, hit the opposite side, ski about half a mile, do a sharp turn, and race down the long last slope. There are red flags all the way to show the route.

The idea is to race against time. It's faster with skis off the ground because there's no friction with the snow. You can do 100 miles an hour that way. But when you've got up speed, the idea is to get on the ground. It's more dangerous. You get points for it. You fly as fast as possible in the air, and stay as long as you dare on the ground.

All the way down, instruments show when the skis are touching the ground. By the time you reach the end, they have the result.

Just before he took off he gave me a wink and said, "See you soon." And when he was half way down the slope someone told me he was a champion.

They didn't have to tell me.

He went like a jet.

He took off normally, and then seemed to vanish. He didn't so much fly the dip as jump it. He hit the other side at colossal speed, and after that I couldn't see him. All I saw was a spray of snow. It did a sharp wiggle at the bend, and then there was something like a vapour trail on the long last slope, and it stopped.

I heard them yelling and jumping all round me.

He returned on the fast cable, and they all started thumping his back, and he was grinning himself. "Not bad," he said, "but not my best. Want to have a try now?" he said to me.

"I don't know," I said.

"We'll do it slowly," he said.

I didn't want to do it any way. I couldn't stop trembling. We had to wait some time, and then he had an argument with the starter. The starter said I didn't have enough experience. I thought he was dead right, and I told him I didn't have any. But Dido said he'd hold me and that I was keen to do it, so the starter said okay and we did it.

"If you wobble, hang on," Dido said.

"Okay," I said.

"You'll manage easily. Switch everything on." He saw that I did. "And remember what I told you. A nice slow start. Bend forward a bit. Everybody's watching. Are you all right?"

"I don't know. I don't think so," I said.

"Yes, you are. You're fine. Bend *forward*." He caught me just as I was wobbling back.

Somehow we got off. He was on the ground, and I was up off it. I started leaning against him, which seemed a good idea, except it unbalanced him, and he had to work hard with his sticks. Also we started going too fast.

"Get on the *ground*," he said. "Put your switches up!"

I was so terrified I couldn't even feel the switches.

"Up!" he said. "*Up*! Like this." He managed to work the switch nearest him.

This brought one ski down and left the other in the air. It also left me hanging round his neck.

"Switch the other one up!" he said. "Get it *up*!"

I found the other switch and got it up, and both skis were on the ground, and I went wobbling there and back, hanging on him, and we were still going downhill, quite fast.

I could see he was mainly afraid of making a fool of himself, so I tried hard and listened to everything he yelled, and somehow we got down the slope. I was hanging on to him all the time.

Before we got to the dip, he put me in the air, and we went gently over it.

Just then I started enjoying it. It was frightening, but it was fun. I'd got the idea, too. You had to crouch forward with your legs bent.

At the other side of the dip he got on the ground himself, but he kept me in the air. He put his arm

73

round me as we rounded the corner flag, and we went into the long last lap. He kept me in the air all the way down it, slowing us by turning his skis in. Somehow we managed it, but right at the end, where there were people waiting, he took his arm away, and I ended up in a heap, with my skis in the air. I couldn't touch ground, and went bobbing about upside down with my skis crossed, and everyone almost collapsed with laughter.

He didn't mind. He was quite proud of me. I hadn't tripped him. I hadn't made a fool of him. He said he'd like to see anyone else try after just half an hour's practice. He said they'd been doing it for forty years. I was beginning to feel pretty good myself then, when he said we could try the real slopes now.

I'd thought these were the real slopes.

He said no, the *real* slopes were at the other side of the mountain. They had the mountain switched on there. They had to, to stop you falling off it.

It was when we got there, and I saw how easy it was to fall off anyway, that I had the feeling I couldn't bear it.

I was beginning to understand him. He was best at everything. It was why he'd gone round and made the speeches. It wasn't because his father was president. He *had* to be best; and he liked danger. Everything he did was dangerous.

I'll say what he did.

THE SWITCHED-ON
MOUNTAIN

e did two runs, very carefully, without trying anything. He pointed out every detail to me.

It's tobogganing. It's power tobogganing. The power comes from the mountain. The toboggan just has the controls. You sit one behind the other, tightly strapped in. You toboggan up the mountain as well as down it. There's an up-track and a down-track.

You go up quite slowly. The toboggan grips the track like a magnet. Coming down, it still grips it tightly, but you're going faster. If you switch off, you're going much faster.

That's the trick. You go as fast as you dare before switching on again. They have the same procedure as on the other side, a starter on top and a judge below. But this way, it's pure speed. You get from top to bottom as fast as you can, in any way you can.

He didn't tell me the various ways you could do it.

He just did the first two runs nice and steady.

He showed me how you worked the toboggan. The front person worked the controls. The back person helped steer, leaning out sideways or back-

75

wards when the toboggan rounded a bend or leaped a hump.

He gave me good warning when I had to do it. He'd yell, "Right!" or "Left!" and I'd lean out to right or left, and we'd swish round the bend without the rear end wobbling. Or if a hump was coming, he'd yell, "Back!" and I'd lean out backwards and we'd sail over and land flat without the nose scooping. (The toboggan is heavier at the front because of the controls.)

At the sharper bends there was a red sign, to give advance warning. But at some of them I saw a yellow sign, with an arrow pointing outwards from the mountain, and I asked why.

He pointed over the side. "Lower track," he said. "You can take a short cut."

Below, I could see the track zig-zagging down the mountain.

Second time round, he showed me the short cut.

Turning sideways at the yellow arrow, you could leave the track, grip tightly to the mountain with power on, and descend to join the next stretch of track below. You could save seconds that way.

He told me when we were going to do it. He yelled, "Back!" and I stretched back as far as I could and we took a slow dive vertically down the mountain.

My head swam.

I was standing upright.

We were stuck like flies to the side of the mountain. I felt my eyes glazing, my body rigid. Yet the moment we hit the lower track and he switched power off and we were whizzing away again, it felt like colossal fun. We did it four or five times, and by the end I was yelling, "Whee!" and laughing as gleefully as he was.

His eyes were shining behind his goggles as we went up for the third run, and he said something to the starter.

"We'll do a timing now," he told me.

I'd forgotten about the timing. He hadn't asked for a timing before.

He started off fast right away, and he didn't even bother putting power on at the first wide bend, just yelled, "Right!" and I swung out and we launched round the bend at speed.

I felt my heart beginning to thud. I could see the red sign ahead for a hairpin bend. It came rushing up in a sickening blur, and he still didn't put power on. He began yelling, "*Left! Left!*" without slackening speed for an instant. I saw, without believing it, that he didn't mean to put power on at all. We were going racing into the hairpin bend. He was leaning out to left himself. I leaned out as far as I could. I leaned so far my head brushed the snow on the banking as we swished in a jackknife curve round it, and levelled out into a wild dangerous wobble, racing from side to side of the icy track as we hurtled down it, not losing speed for an instant.

I could hear him cackling in front. I could see another red sign coming up, with a yellow one.

"Dido!" I yelled. "Slow down!"

He couldn't hear me. The wind snatched my words away. I could hear him, though. He was yelling, "Back!"

Back? He meant left. I had to bend *left* again. Another tight hairpin was coming. It was almost here.

"*Back*!" he yelled. "*Back*!" and started straining back himself, so I did, too.

He didn't turn into the bend. He followed the yellow arrow. He went full speed off the mountain.

I thought my heart had stopped.

We were in the air, off the mountain.

Just as we lost contact, he snapped power on. I felt the magnet clamp tight. We fell and hit the lower track hard, and the instant we did so, he let power off, and we were still going at terrific speed.

I couldn't bear it. I wanted to get out. I wanted to get off.

He was cackling like a lunatic in front.

I followed blindly whatever he said. "*Left*!" "*Right*!" "*Back*!" We skated madly round the banking. We flew through the air over humps.

We came to another arrow.

"*Back*!"

Again we flew off the mountain. I wanted to close my eyes, but didn't dare. I was straining back, waiting for the thud of power to come on. It came on, and I clenched my toes, waiting for the thump. There was no thump. Almost immediately, he let power off again. The lower track sailed past us, and we were still dropping. He let one track, two tracks, flash past, before bringing on power, and we landed on the third. He switched power off just as we landed, but we did it with such a thud we leaped clear in the air, a good five feet, still scudding down at breakneck pace.

I'd practically given up now. I wasn't even sure when it ended. We were stopped. People were jumping and yelling. The judge was checking the figures.

He was checking them again. I hadn't even got out of the toboggan. I was still strapped in.

"Well. Not bad," Dido said. He'd shoved his goggles up, and was grinning. "Second best time for eighty years. What do you say to that?"

I didn't say anything.

"Barry?" he said. He seemed to be looking at me closely.

Then I was in a hut, and he was giving me tigra.

"Are you all right?" he said.

I still couldn't speak.

"Barry?"

I sipped the tigra. I felt better every second.

"Didn't you like it?" he said.

"I hated it," I said. "Don't do it again. Never do *anything* like that with me again."

He just blinked at me.

"Have a nap," he said. "It's time for one now."

I asked him about it later. I asked about the danger. I asked if it wasn't possible to be killed in Egon.

He said of course you could be killed. If you smashed yourself badly, you were killed.

So he knew. He knew what could happen.

THE LAKE BEGINS
TO GLOW

had to put that to show what he's like.
The place isn't like that. Their lives aren't like that.
It's all fun there. I'll say what it's like, after a nap.

You have a nap. I didn't even want a nap. He said
I had to. It's for your body. They sleep the exact time
they want. They always know the time. It's in their
brains. If they want to sleep eight and a quarter
hours, they sleep exactly eight and a quarter hours.

We slept five minutes. Then he woke me, and I
was dizzy.

It's the air. You find you're smiling. You can't stop
it. You do stop after a bit, but you keep on inside.
You feel your inside smiling.

We took a walk. He said we'd got our kites booked
for later. I could see the kites out over the lake. I
could see people in fish suits playing with fish under
water. There were groups of people relaxing in water
clubs. They were in floating armchairs, chatting or
reading. Food tables were floating between them.

From the jetties, every kind of entertainment was
going on. There was swimming and sailing and acro-
batic diving and bat diving, with wings. There were

things I'd never seen before. There was a Big Wheel, like at a fair, that whirled you up in the air and then round under water. There were kids with spring floats on their feet jumping on the lake like water insects.

In the pleasure gardens other things went on. There were games and music and performances of various kinds. But we ate just then. There were thousands of eating places and foam-ice places. I didn't put anything about foam-ice.

It's ice cream. You have to call it that, except it's a hundred times better. It squirts out of a machine and turns into foam, fantastically creamy. They have it in over ninety flavours. You have it with portions of nuts, or chocolate, or various kinds of crunches, or raisins and mandaro (it's a kind of peel, like jelly). Or you have it with hot or cold fudge, or soft or semi-soft toffee. There are thousands of combinations.

Also there are foam-ice chews. They're in wrappers that keep them compressed and frozen till you open them. It's an incredible sensation when you chew the hard bar and it swells into foam-ice in your mouth. Or you can get them in assortments, like little wrapped toffees, in a bag.

We had some foam-ice. Then we ate. We ate pansa patty. I mainly ate that. It's a hamburger, though I never tasted a hamburger like it. You pick what shade you want it cooked, from a shade card. You can have it from pink to dark brown. You can have it from soft to crisp. There's no grease. You have it with chips and salad, and with any of about twenty or thirty sauces that you put on yourself.

The meat is sensational, except it isn't meat. They don't eat meat. They don't eat fish, either, or any other creature. They understand the creatures and communicate with them, so it would be like eating people. Anyway, he said there was no sense in eating them.

He said when you ate a steak all you were eating was grass that a cow had processed. He said you didn't have to kill the cow to get at the steak. You could make the steak, the same way the cow did. You could make anything, and they did. They made an unbelievable number of foods. They made more foods than people above ever knew, including all the ones they did know, and every one I tasted was better.

It grew dark as we ate, and I saw the lake begin to glow. It glowed purple from underneath. The ragusa trees began to glow.

I felt fantastic. I'd only slept five minutes but I felt I'd slept all night. I felt I'd just woken up, on holiday, full of sun and fresh air, and wanting to do everything in the world.

We strolled along and met other kids. He said we'd do a pleasure drome next, but we'd do it after a ragusa. Second ragusa time was coming up.

There were over a hundred of us in the garden when we had our ragusas this time. We swung in our hammocks, and ate our ragusas, and couldn't stop laughing, and again it was unbelievable.

There was the glow in the trees. There were the stars up above.

I looked at the stars, and wondered.

He hadn't explained the stars yet, or the sun and moon. He'd explained hardly anything.

And I haven't myself yet, though I knew more by then. I knew a lot more. I just can't tell it yet. Except

I'll tell one thing. You read stories and you see films. They show you the future, and it's creepy. It's a terrible future with frightening people and mad-looking places. And they've got it wrong. I've been there, and it's great. It's a future full of fun. It's supposed to be. There's a reason for it, and I'll tell it.

But right then I was swinging in my hammock, laughing at the stars, and not knowing that trouble was coming. But it was coming pretty soon.

THE PLEASURE DROME

The trouble started at the pleasure drome where the manager didn't want to let me in. He said the pleasure was so strong it could burst my brain. He said I might be able to bear the next show, which was for small kids of seventy and eighty, and he'd think about it.

We waited, and saw the people from the last show start coming out, and this was when I noticed their feet weren't touching the ground. They came floating out, and they were smiling. They had the weird kind of smiles that angels have in pictures.

We didn't bother asking the manager. We just sneaked in, to the big hall. There were rows of seats circling a central space. There was no stage or screen. There was just a space, with a green carpet. It took a few minutes for everyone to settle. Then the lights went out and some of the kids started whispering, and some of the others told them to shut up.

Nothing happened for a bit, then I realised that in the dark I could see the green carpet, and that it wasn't a carpet but the sea. It was bigger than I thought it was. It was higher than I thought it was. It was all round me and up to my chin, and I could feel it. It was past my chin. I was under it. There was green water all round me.

My heart was thumping, and I heard the kids squealing. I felt Dido hanging on my arm. "It's okay," he said in my ear.

We were under water and breathing. I put out my tongue and tasted the sea. I could hear it surging. I could hear it whistling, and singing. It was uncanny singing, without words. It was a low moan going all the way up to a high shriek. It was unearthly and beautiful. It was like no music I'd ever heard; fascinating, of another world.

"Whales," Dido whispered in my ear. "The whales are singing."

And suddenly, in a colossal great smother of foam, three of them sprang up; massive whales, at least eighty feet long. They flashed past me, and I saw the whole length of them, mouths to tails, and swung round in my seat, and saw them fanning off in the sea all round. All the sea was lashed into luminous foam, and I heard the kids squealing, and saw their arms flickering up under water like seaweed to try and touch the whales.

There was a fantastic volume of sound as the whales tore round and sang, and spiralled upwards, and we went up with them; up and up through glorious green depths, with the water suddenly sparkling and lightening, until we burst right out of it, and the whales blew.

They blew huge spouts of water. We were cascading in the air with their spouts, and then had left them behind.

They were far behind, far below.

I could see them below; three whales, flicking their fantails on the surface of the sea: tiny whales now, because we were going fast. We were going at fantastic speed. We were rushing through the air, and all the kids were squealing again because all round the blue sky was whistling with our speed, and we were in the world above.

My brain was spinning. The world was spinning. I could see it below me, and our rocket dizzyingly turned, so that the world lurched upwards, until it was level, and I could see its curve. I saw the curve of the earth. I saw tiny mountains standing up, like on a relief globe. The globe slowly spun. I saw Spain, and France. I saw Britain. I saw the finger of Cornwall. I saw where Polziel must be!

I saw ocean and Canada and the eastern coast of America all the way down to Florida; the whole shape of it slowly turning, until the distance was too great, and no detail could be seen, just the whole globe turning, turning. And also turning blue.

The globe was blue now: a beautiful little planet, enclosed in its atmosphere, receding fast, at hundreds of thousands of miles an hour.

It was whistling darkness now as the planet contracted into a tiny sapphire, into a bit of diamond dust, into nothing.

The kids had stopped squealing. In the rushing darkness, there was a kind of awe, and the rocket slowly revolved once more, and a little bright star passed on our left, with a tiny scatter of dust about it, and Dido said in my ear, "The sun. The solar system." And it was gone.

All gone. Everything was gone. There was nothing anywhere. There was no light. There was a roaring darkness, that was thudding, and thudding rhythmically. It was thudding like a heart. It was my heart. All of me was thudding, my feet, my hands, my hair. I was a part of the thudding. I was suddenly a part of everything, of the whole universe, of space. I was smaller than my own pulse. I was a beat in everything's pulse. I didn't exist. I hadn't been born. It was all blackness.

It was fantastic blackness.

I'd never known such blackness. I couldn't see any of myself. I couldn't even feel myself. I couldn't believe the blackness. In the darkest room, on the darkest night, behind closed eyes, you couldn't see such blackness. If you stared hard enough you could always see something, a fleck.

I stared as hard as I could. I stared so hard my eyes ached, but I got a fleck. I got a spark. It was like a pain. It was red so I knew it was blood from the veins behind my eyes. Then it grew bigger, and I knew it wasn't.

The spark was there. It hung in the blackness. It was brighter than a cigarette end, redder than a ruby. It was bigger than an egg, than a balloon, than the moon. It wasn't even red. In the thudding vibrations, it was changing colour. It was rose, and pink, apricot, peach, pearl. In steady throbbing waves it expanded everywhere.

It washed over the front rows, and I heard the gasps of delight and saw the kids standing up; and felt it coming towards me, and got the first tremor myself. The sound was changing, too. The light was washing the harshness out of it. It was melting and softening into music. Then it touched me and a single great gasp came out of me. I felt I was just born, out of nothing. I felt I was a baby being bathed. I felt I was being picked up. And unbelievably I was. The kids in front weren't standing. The light had lifted them. We were all floating in it.

Now there were all colours, blue, silver, amber, emerald, and they were rippling through me. The colours and the sounds were going through me. I seemed to be shimmering in long ripples of pleasure. They got so intense, they came so fast, I could hardly bear it. Just when I couldn't bear it, and heard myself gasping again, a clear tide of sapphire blue washed through me.

Everywhere the kids were gently floating. Dido was floating beside me. We were all smiling the weird smiles; we couldn't help it. I don't know how long it went on. There were several more of the spasms. They got stronger. The feeling of happiness was almost painful. Then it became softer and gentler, till we were lowered to our seats again, and there was a smell of flowers everywhere. I could smell them as we went bobbing out into the night. I couldn't feel the ground. It was like treading water. I was just full of pleasure.

I was so full of it I forgot to tell him again not to do anything dangerous with me.

And my time had come now. It was here.

MY TIME HAS COME

It was the middle of the night.

We were soaring.

We'd soared so high, the lake, far below, looked no bigger than a plum itself. The smell of ragusas was everywhere in the purple night. I didn't ever want it to stop.

There'd never been anything so beautiful.

The pleasure drome hadn't been so beautiful.

I was lying on the kite just gazing below. The moon was over Mount Julas. I was higher than Mount Julas. I could see the snow in the moonlight. And we were still rising. The scented air wafted up from the lake. I could feel the soft gusts trembling each wing under my body. It only needed a touch to correct the wings.

We'd gone up first in a dual-control kite, and he'd shown me everything. He knew I was nervous, but he said there was nothing to it. And it was true. In just minutes he'd let me take control myself. You take off under power, nose upwards. Then a few hundred feet up, you level out, and feel the air currents underneath, and switch off. The air takes you then.

Now we were on our own, and he was soaring twenty feet away. There were fifty of us over the lake, the maximum at night; some were already stunting and spiralling below. The kites flashed like fireflies in the moonlight. Far below, just a few hundred feet off the water, I saw somebody trying a slice. He did it cautiously, but pretty well. He levelled out just at the right moment, and then he was coming up again, under power.

Dido just laughed. "Some slice!" he said scornfully. "I'll have to show him. You stay here. Stabilise now. You remember how."

He took me through it, and we both stabilised.

It isn't hovering. You lock into position magnetically. You stay in one spot in the air. I felt the breeze on the wings but it couldn't shift the kite even fractionally.

He de-stabilised and slipped away slightly in the air, and hovered awhile, and I saw him tightening his straps.

"Okay," he said.

He put the kite on its nose and took off like a bullet. He went so fast I knew he was on full power. Just a few hundred feet below he went into a slice! It's fantastically dangerous. At that height it's almost lunacy. He put the kite on its side so that he was slicing down like a knife. I saw him spread-eagled along the kite. In that position you can barely judge distance or direction. He'd explained all this to me! And I'd seen it. With power off, you've got practically no control. You can't maneuver the wings. If you're in trouble you need lightning reactions to snap on power again. And you can be in trouble in an instant. A sudden gust can throw you all over the sky. It can break the kite and snap you in two. It's why they'd all done it so cautiously and just a few hundred feet over the lake, where the air currents were manageable and they could judge distance.

The lunatic was doing it from two miles up.

And he'd got power *off* now, I could see. The thin knife edge of his kite gave a fast dangerous twirl every second or two. I could hear it whistling. Far below, the others could, too. I saw them swooping out of the way as his kite sliced down through the night, shrieking like a siren.

About a mile below a gust caught him. He spun completely round in the air, twice, fluttering like a moth. I could imagine him fighting for the controls, everything spinning fast round him. It didn't stop him for a moment. He didn't level out; he didn't slow. He got control, must have snapped on power for a second, and continued slicing down.

He wasn't going to make it. He'd misjudged. He was going fast, much too fast. He was almost in the water.

He was in it! He'd crashed. He'd misjudged and smashed himself in the water. I saw a huge column of spray leap up. And on top of it, there he was! He must have been just a few inches off the water when he snapped on power and levelled out. He'd been within a fraction of an inch of killing himself.

I lay on my kite, two miles up, and trembled. He was mad. He was dangerous. I was frightened to touch any of the controls, even accidentally.

I lay in the sky and watched him come shooting up. He did a complete victory roll round me, and

90

finished upside down, exactly above. He locked in position there and looked down at me, grinning.

"How was it?" he said. His face was a yard above mine, eyes shining. He was just breathing a bit hard.

"It was mad!" I said.

He laughed and leaned down and rumpled my hair.

"It was *fun*," he said. He unlocked and made a slow semicircle to stabilise beside me, and we lay in silence for a while, looking below.

"All life's fun," he said. "It's supposed to be. Don't you feel it?"

"Not when it's dangerous," I said.

"There's no danger. Trust me."

I said, "You don't know what's dangerous. You don't know what it is to be frightened."

"I won't frighten you. I promise," he said. "Do you want to do a couple of rolls now?"

"No," I said.

"You'll love it. We'll do it *gently*," he said.

He took me through the controls again.

The kite was a long triangle. You lay along the spine, strapped on, looking down on either side of the narrow point. The wings were of a thin metal, with moveable flaps. You controlled them with a rudder bar and a nose stick. The bar steered you to left or right, and the stick brought the nose up or down.

Beside the controls was the switch panel. The first switch was for the force line, and I'd got it on so I couldn't crash. The next was power with a turnable grip to control the speed. Last was the stabiliser lock. You could lock in any position. You could do it upside down, as he'd just done. You could stand the kite on its nose, or tail, and it would stay there. He'd told me to keep my hands away from it in flight, because it stopped you instantly, faster than the brakes of any car.

We put all switches off, and did a slow spiralling descent.

He did it carefully, bringing us down gently: sticks slightly forward to keep the nose down, rudder bars gently to the right.

It was the most beautiful, graceful thing. We curved down and down through the purple night.

We stopped before we came to the group below.

"There's nothing to a roll, Barry," he said. "The kite does *everything*. If you're nervous, do it on power."

He did one, very slowly, to show me, and then another. He carefully looped the loop round me. The second time, he locked, just as he went into the loop, and stayed there slanting in the air, to show me how he'd got the controls.

There *was* nothing to it. You pulled the stick pretty far back to get into a steep climb. Just as the kite went vertical, you pulled the stick farther back, which carried it round in a circle, and you were upside down. As you came down the circle, you pushed the stick forward to level out; and as you levelled, you pulled it back again.

I tried it, very cautiously, bracing myself to lock if anything went wrong. Nothing went wrong. I did the most fantastic, gorgeous, incredible roll in the air. The whole world spun, and I hung upside down in it, and slid down the other side, hooting with joy. I did another. The sky was under me, the glowing lake up in the sky.

I just didn't want to stop doing it. But I was doing it on power—slow power—and I knew I'd have to do it without. It was what they were doing below, with several fancy tricks. He hovered, carefully watching me. He called out, "Okay. Lock," and drifted over and locked beside me.

"It's the same movement without power," he said, "only you come down faster. You pull back quicker on the stick. If you get confused, go on slow power and lock."

He did it himself, to show me, calling out all the time. He did it slowly, but it still wasn't as slow as before; and then I was doing it myself.

He drifted away to give me room, and I unlocked. I put the nose up and started the ascent. When I was vertical I pulled the stick back farther, and immediately flipped over on my back. I slid down the circle fast, very fast, and immediately began pushing the stick forward, and evened out, and went right up again.

The first time I was so petrified I barely knew what I was doing. The second time I began to feel it. There was the breeze in my ears, the wings suddenly alive under me. After that, I went crazy. Every time I flipped, the blood rushed to my head, the lake was where the sky should be, and I let out a great hoot. I slid down the sky and heard myself cackling the way he'd cackled in the toboggan.

I was a bird. I had wings. I was flying in the night.

It's the thing I remember best. It's still the thing I remember best, even after my death. And that wasn't far off now. It was there, minutes later. It was in the air.

DYING

I remember the moment it happened. I remember when everything went wrong, and I couldn't put it right. It happened below, way below. It was past where the skychasing was going on. He took me there when he saw I could handle the kite, and we joined in.

It's a game, sky-chasing. You form a circle, with the chaser in the middle. You switch on the kite's computer, and also the force line. When the game begins you "scramble" and the chaser starts chasing. He has to make "hits." He can't really hit. The force line stops him. But when he's near enough, the computer scores a hit.

It happens in a space called the "box." You mustn't fly out of the box. If you do the computer scores a hit against you for that, too. It scores everything.

The games are fast and tight, inside the box. Everyone gets a turn. And everyone scored off me. And I scored off nobody. I was terrible.

I was so terrible, Dido took me out of it, to show

me some of the tricks to use. He took me well below the box. We went to seven or eight hundred feet. He showed me the flip and the slide and the drop. I was scared of all of them. He did them on full power. The game was on full power, which had confused me, anyway. The speed had confused me.

The flip is a fast drop-turn. You drop and immediately turn in a way the chaser doesn't expect. He acted as chaser, and he said I had to keep changing the turn. I had to do it faster and faster. He made so many hits, he got irritable. He shouted, "*Change* your turn!" And just the moment he said it, I turned the same way, and he made another hit, and he yelled, "Again! Try again!" And I did it again, and found I was turning the same way again. It was all so fast. It was too fast for me. Just as I did it, he yelled, "Not that way!" And I slammed the rudder bar over, and that's when it happened.

I slammed it too hard. The kite went into a spin. I was on full power, so it spun like a top. I couldn't shift the rudder bar. I'd spun thirty or forty times when I started being sick. My eyes were glazed with fright, my fists clenched, my whole body hunched together like one terrified muscle. I blacked out for a moment, but when I came to, everything was still spinning: sky, moon, lake . . . sky-moon-lake . . . skymoonlake. It wouldn't stop.

He'd got as close as he could. He was yelling at me. I heard only snatches of words. "Rudder . . . Leave it . . . Power . . . *Get on slow power!*"

I got my hands off the rudder, and fought against the spin to find the switch panel. My eyes were full of tears and I couldn't see the panel. Everything kept spinning. I felt for the switches, found power, gripped the handle to slow it, and turned hard. I turned off! I'd switched it off.

It slowed me right away. I had the rudder right away. I yanked it over fast. I came out of the spin, with a huge strain on the wings, and on my straps, and was vertical. I thought I was vertical. It took three or four seconds, my head still going round and round, to find that I wasn't vertical. I was sideways. I was in a slice.

I pulled frantically this way and that on the rudder. The rudder worked, but the wings didn't. I remembered you had no control of them in a slice. I heard them begin to whistle. I hung sideways on the kite and cut down through the night. I saw the lake seven hundred feet below. It was purple. It was transparent.

I saw fish below the surface. I saw people in fish suits. He was plummeting down beside me, shouting. I was too paralysed to do anything.

He shouted, "Barry—get on power! *Switch on power!*"

Sobbing, I tried to do it. I couldn't take my eyes off the lake. It was close now, three hundred feet, two hundred. I could hear a gurgling noise coming out of me. I felt for the panel, and counted off levers, and switched on power. Just the moment I did it, I knew it was wrong. It wasn't power. It was the stabiliser lock. I was just feet off the water. I was maybe inches off it. I felt a terrific wrench. I felt something like a wall slam into me. Then for a time there was nothing. I'd entered death.

WHO AM I NOW?

Polziel, Cornwall, August 18.

I'm too tired to write today. I've written too many days. Writing of my death tired me.

I've been wondering who I am; if I'm the same person I was before I died. I know the body is the same. But is the mind? They played so many tricks with my mind. I wonder if it's the one I had before.

I know he said you couldn't make a mind. He said only the brain made a mind. But if the brain was changed, even accidentally, wouldn't it make a different mind?

I kept asking him last night. I was down there till three in the morning.

I've got the cave tidied up now. The steps are mainly cleared. I can get down in minutes. I keep a few things there. I keep a bit of food and a towel (for when I go in the flooded tunnel). I keep a spare flashlight and a rope. I've tied a noose in the rope, and hammered a bolt in the cliff, so I can lasso it and pull myself up if I get stuck by the sea. I don't want them finding out I'm missing and coming to look for me. I've got to be careful.

I know so much. I see things so differently.

I look at my parents, and I feel older than them. I feel older than anyone. I know more than they'll ever know. The whole world seems childish and ignorant. I feel I've stepped back a thousand years; as if they haven't invented clockwork yet or engines, radio or flight, and can't even imagine such things.

I have seen greater things! I've seen the future, and it's wonderful. The world is wonderful, and the universe. The idea behind it is wonderful.

What do they know of these things? How can I begin telling them? I feel lost, and out of my time. But I won't stay this way. I know what to do.

It's strange that I knew more after I died than before. I knew almost everything.

I'll rest today. I'll write tomorrow what I knew.

WHAT I KNEW

knew I was under trees. I knew I was on the ground. I didn't know I'd died. I couldn't feel anything. The body on the ground seemed disconnected from me.

It wasn't alone. Two people were with it. One was Dido. He said, "Is he dead?"

The other said, "He's suspended."

Dido said, "Did he have pain?"

"Feel."

I understood all this. Either they were talking English or I understood everything now. Dido's hand went to the body on the ground, and suddenly it was my body, and it was my head he was touching, and I felt all the body and the pain in it. But still I felt disconnected. I realised I *was* disconnected. I was in somebody's hand. My brain was in the other person's hand. The pain moaned in the body's shoulder and neck. I realised a part of me was doing the moaning. I saw that Dido was, too. His face was screwed up in a great grimace. The pain lasted only a few seconds; and then he had taken his hand away and the pain went; but the grimace stayed on his face. He was still feeling my pain.

"That's what you did to him," the other person said, and everything went away again. I went away. I went back in the hand. Then I went to a hammock.

"Barry," Dido said. He was standing beside the hammock, watching me.

I didn't say anything.

"Forgive me," Dido said.

I still didn't say anything. I was waiting for the pain. There was no pain.

"You're all right. You're resting," Dido said. "You have to rest another hour."

I saw the sky was lighter. I was in the hotel garden. I seemed to hear what he said before he said it. (It was why my mind needed resting. A part of the brain heard what he said and passed it to another part. I was only understanding the second part of the brain, like getting an echo before the original. But by the time it was in my mind it had already become familiar. My mind was confused because its brain had been taken out and handled after death.)

I'd died on the kite. I was dead when they got to me. I'd broken my neck and my shoulder. The doctor had seen it happen and had treated me immediately. The heart had stopped, but he'd found oxygen still in the brain, so he had kept it there and restarted the heart. He had kept me "suspended" between life and death while he looked to see if it was worth giving me my life back. He had treated the shoulder first to see if there were difficulties, and there weren't. He'd healed the break instantly. Then he'd repaired the broken connections between the spine and the brain before mending the neck itself.

He'd said if these parts had been damaged beyond repair, he'd have had to "let me go." He couldn't replace my parts. They had different parts. We were of different species.

Dido told me the difference. (Either then or later, he told me.) He told me why they had no pain.

He said I had pain to warn that something was wrong with my body. It was like a fuse in an electric system. If something went wrong, the fuse blew to protect the system. If I cut my hand, it hurt to warn that I'd damaged a part that could endanger my body—from loss of blood or infection. I could cut other parts of my body, that didn't endanger it, and they wouldn't hurt. I could cut my hair or my fingernails, and they wouldn't hurt.

He said that with them everything was like hair and fingernails. No part of them could hurt. They always knew the state of their bodies in the same way that they always knew the time. He said right at that moment he could feel his brain and his kidneys and his liver. Nothing could go wrong with them that he wouldn't know about, and nobody in Egon could die of illness.

I asked him what they did die of.

He said they died if they broke vital parts that couldn't be replaced in time, or of old age.

I asked why old age mattered if illness didn't.

He said it had to do with Egon.

We weren't talking then. We were using brain waves, to rest my mind. He'd told me about it. He said they used speech socially, but they didn't need to. With animals they only used brain waves. He said I was like an animal. I had a mind a bit like a dog's. A dog's mind was simple but interesting, because it knew more than you thought it knew. He said it was fun getting in a dog's mind when it dreamed. A part of you became the dog, to understand it. A part of him had just become me to understand me.

He said the word "Egon" meant "life." Or it could mean "mind." He couldn't find the right word in my head. He said everything was a part of Egon, but a person's particular part was called his "ego," and it wore out. It wasn't a physical thing so you couldn't replace it.

He said Egon didn't mean just the world of Egon. The world of Egon was part of a larger Egon. The larger Egon was the galaxy of worlds, and earth was just an ego in it.

He saw I didn't understand.

He said I'd better not try just now.

He said I *would* understand. I'd understand when we had the last experience, and I'd rested long enough now, so we could have it.

The last experience was under Plum Lake.

This was the one he hadn't any words for.
I think we went down then.
I think I learnt the lot down there.

THE TIMELESS CAVERNS

You don't swim down. You take an elevator. The elevators go direct from the jetties to the caverns. There are scores of caverns, all connected. They have another world there. It's a world of beautiful light. There's a sky, and clouds, and some of the clouds almost bob on the ground. It's always spring or autumn, according to the part you're in. You can go from spring to autumn and then into spring again.

They have fantastic scenery in the caverns. There are wide landscapes with valleys and meadows, connected by winding paths with waterfalls and grottoes. There are airlocks through all the caverns to keep the water out. The air you breathe is from the springs.

It's a dreamland there. Fish swim in the air. You swim in it, or float. You take a weight-belt down with you, and to walk you have to pick up rocks and put them in your belt.

The first thing you notice is that time has slowed.

It's so slow, it almost stops. You feel your ideas forming. You feel each thought happening.

We came to a clearing, and I saw angels sitting on a cloud, playing harps. Then I looked again, and it was giants, playing guitars. They were lounging on the cloud with their guitars.

I couldn't move away. I just wanted to stay and listen. The notes didn't fade in the air. The old notes hung in the air with the new ones. The music seemed to go on for ever, like bells. But Dido drew me on. He drew me off the trail, up a hillside. We floated up. We floated into a grotto, and weighted ourselves, and drank from the pool there.

He began telling me things without speaking.

Everything got slower. His thoughts got slower.

They were so slow, so simple, I found myself looking all over the thoughts, and examining them.

He showed me Egon, and other worlds, and we drank more from the pool.

Time practically stopped. There was so much time, it seemed limitless. Every moment came slowly along like a huge landscape, and in every part of it something was happening.

I saw all history. I saw the distant past. I saw the world as one continent: its beautiful scenery, its glittering cities, its soundless rockets speeding between the cities and the stars. Then he showed me the present, and the people in the world above, huddled on their mountains and worrying. They worried about everything, the cost of things, their health, the danger of attack by other people. It was the present but it was so crude and primitive it looked remoter than the past.

He brought it closer for me, and I saw myself

being born. I saw myself as a baby. I saw everything I'd ever done. I've no time to put it now. They stop time there, so I couldn't tell it was passing; but he said it was, anyway, and we had to move.

We moved to spring (it's autumn in the grottoes), and he told me the reason for the caverns. You stop your life there. You stop it where you want. You enter your mind and look at all you've ever done.

In autumn you do it to see where your life has reached and to find out what you missed (because it's all there, even things you didn't notice at the time). And in spring you do it for fun, because everything is new again. Every sensation in the world becomes new. All the colours, the smells, the tastes, everything you ever felt, you feel for the first time again.

It's lemon and primrose, the light in spring.

I nearly went out of my mind in spring.

We were in meadows sparkling with flowers. We were nosing through trees heavy with blossom. We were jumping, flying, rolling everywhere, and my senses reeled. I felt I'd been given the world to play in. I felt I'd been given my body as a present. I couldn't believe I owned my body. It seemed a fantastic thing to own. It could do so much and feel so much, and every part of it was marvellous. The whole world was marvellous. I couldn't take in enough of it. I couldn't breathe enough, or see or smell or hear enough.

But he kept drawing me on. He said there was so much to do, and not much time to do it now.

We did the jubal-racing, and the fishing. We went out of the caverns to the lake, and then back in, and I learned the lot.

First, the jubals: a jubal is a shark, a racing shark,

and you ride it. Then fishing. In fishing, you don't catch fish. You become a fish. It's unbelievable. But even before that, there was him. He'd changed towards me. He'd changed since he thought he'd ended my life and felt my pain.

Before, he'd treated me like a pet, like something to show off. But now he seemed . . . to love me. It's hard to explain it. I don't even understand it. But he wouldn't leave me for a moment. He kept looking at me and I felt him thinking my thoughts. And I suddenly realised something else. I saw that though he acted like a kid and could feel like a kid, he was old. He was a very old man. He was older than my grandparents, older than anyone I knew or had even heard of. He was looking after me.

He wouldn't let me go in for the jubal-racing, so he didn't himself. We just watched, and I saw why he'd stopped me.

They do it in the pure spring water. They have a race course that twists and turns, and it's full of the bubbling water. The sharks go crazy in it. They're trapped into five separate pens while the riders are lowered into the saddles and strapped on. Then the traps are raised, and the sharks take off. They take off like an explosion, and until the first bend you can't even see them. All you see is flying water, with something like five torpedoes in front. Then at the bend the course narrows so that they can't go round in a line and the tricks start.

A shark is so fast and powerful it reacts like lightning in any water. But in spring water, it's dynamite. All you could see was exploding water and torpedo shapes with riders bent flat over them. The riders were communicating with the sharks all the time, getting them to leap or dive, or even twist round to block other riders. And the orders had to be right the first time, for the sharks obeyed immediately, giving no chance for a change of mind.

They went hurtling round the bend—under water, or on it, or even out of it—and hit the next wide stretch, and a frantic struggle started. The obstacles began here—tunnels, and walls of rock that had to be leapt, and waterfalls that had to be dived. The sharks could go as fast as each other, so it wasn't just a battle of speed; it was a battle of wits—and of nerve.

We were on a platform over the course, so we could see the whole thing; and I saw him jumping and twitching and clenching his fists, and I knew he wanted to race himself, so I told him to do it. But he said he wouldn't. He said we'd go fishing now.

We got our fish suits—they have them in all sizes—and floated horizontally while they were fitted. They fit them very tightly. They fit gloves on your fingers and on your toes. They fit you into the exact shape of the suit, with every part of you in contact with it. It's a suit the shape of a fish, with a skin a quarter of an inch thick that has all the equipment. It has everything a fish has. It has scales and gills and fins and a tail, and every movement you make is translated into the movement a fish makes. The gills open and shut to let the water flow, and the equipment takes the air from it for you to breathe. You don't breathe a special way, like in a mask. You just breathe.

He gave me a practice to see I'd got it, and we floated round awhile in the air. Then he led the way to an airlock, and we went through. We went through to the bottom of the lake.

I thought I had to be dreaming.

It was totally incredible.

It was like purple glass. It was like a purple glass lens. It was so clear I could see all twelve miles of it, from one end to the other. I could see right up in the sky, with the skydivers circling high above. Even stranger, I could see both sides of me at once. I could see like a fish. I was a fish.

Right away I was acting like a fish. I was making all the darting movements a fish makes. Every tiny movement of mine was converted into the powerful muscular motion of a fish. I could feel fish communicating all round me. I could feel Dido communicating with them. Everything came clear through the suit.

I heard him laughing and he yelled, "Come on!" and did a streak up the lake. I streaked up it with him. I did a streak of about three miles, without any feeling of tiredness, and only stopped then because I couldn't stop laughing. It's the gas. You feel crazy. You feel totally unreal. The world under the lake is round, round as a goldfish bowl, and you can see everything at once.

I felt freer than a bird there, freer than anything. I was flying, in water; doing whatever I wanted, without effort. And all my life was with me, all the moments that had happened and all the moments happening now, and every one of them seemed magic. I had a dizzy feeling I was seeing it for the first time; that all my life had been a game and I'd been playing it without knowing.

A school of fish had streaked up with us, and they began playing with us. But we didn't seem to have done it more than a few minutes when he said we had to go. He said the gas was deceiving me, and we'd done it for hours, and now there was hardly any time left at all. He said we'd return to the caverns and he'd tell me everything now, and maybe I'd understand.

So we did, and he told me.

And I wish he hadn't now. I wish I hadn't heard it.

THE BILLIONS OF WORLDS

He said there were a thousand million stars in our galaxy, many with worlds. He said outside our galaxy there were a million million other galaxies, all with worlds, billions upon billions of worlds, like ours.

He said our world was a ball of rock, and everything we had came out of the rock: the sea, the atmosphere, all the plants and creatures. They were made of it. Hot molten material had come out of the rock and the steam from it had formed the sea, and the minerals in the sea had formed life; all from the rock.

He said it was still going on. The creation hadn't finished. The earth kept reproducing itself like any of the creatures it made. It kept making new material, which came up as molten rock and nudged aside old used-up material, pushing it under again for remelting. When it nudged a "plate" carrying land you got earthquakes. But mainly you didn't because most of the earth was under water, so it mostly happened there.

He said people above hardly knew about it yet. He said they knew hardly anything. He knew everything they knew above, and everything they ever *had* known. He told me how he knew it. He told me about their education in Egon.

He said until they were sixty, they hardly had any. They just had sport and art. They learned all the sports and all the arts. (That's why they could do everything.) He said these were creative things so they had to be *learned*; you couldn't get them any other way, and it was all you actually did learn. Everything else was programmed direct to your brain. You got reading and writing fed to your brain, then communications and sciences and languages.

He said there was only one language in Egon, but they did everybody else's. They did all the languages of the planet, and of animals, and of other planets. He said he'd got all French in half an hour and all the dialects of Asia in a week. He knew every language there'd ever been.

I asked him what use they were, and he said none, but they didn't have to be, because once you started thought training you could use any language, anyway. He'd only had to touch my head and he knew all mine. And when he was older he wouldn't even have to do that; he'd just look at a person and know it. But you got the programmes to work your brain and grow your mind. That was the point of them, and actually it was the point of your life.

He said your mind *was* your life, so the bigger one you could grow the more "life" you had. He said people above didn't understand it because they never grew up. They just grew old too fast, and died while they were children, with children's minds.

He said their baby smashed violins because it was a baby, and all kids acted in a crazy way. But when their minds shaped up, at seventy or eighty, they began growing out of it; except people above couldn't because they didn't live enough yet to grow the right kind of mind.

He said cave men had the same kind of minds people had today, and they thought they knew everything. People always thought that. He said ten thousand years ago they thought it, and twenty thousand years ago. When you looked back you saw they knew practically nothing. And what they knew was mainly useless. Every few years they learned something that changed most of what they knew before.

He said it had been the same in Egon. Egon had been discovered by a scientist called Glister, and they'd called the Glister Deep after him. He'd first discovered the Deep and under it the Abyss, and then a way through that to the caves of Egon. He'd been looking for energy materials that hadn't yet come out of the earth. They'd still used earth for their energy then, and it was millions of years before they learned how to plug in directly to the sun.

He said it was millions of years more before even the sun's energy wasn't enough and they thought they had to move to a bigger star. And it wasn't till after the mess-up, when the world had been remade in Egon, that they learned they didn't need stars, either. Even the stars had to get their energy from somewhere. . . .

Everything he said, I was understanding. He wasn't even saying it. He just thought, and I knew it. He was showing me their sciences. He showed me light science.

He said radio was a branch of light science. He said just as you sat in a house and tuned in the radio, you could sit and tune in light. You could do it anywhere. It's how they had the sun, moon, and stars under the sea. They had the receivers fixed high in the roof of Egon. They had them tuned in directly above so that as the earth turned they had night and day and all the seasons.

He said you didn't have to tune in to right above, or even to the present time. You could tune in to any time, to anywhere. He said when you saw a star, you were seeing how it looked hundreds or thousands of years ago. It took that long for its light to reach earth. The light didn't stop because you saw some on earth. It kept going past earth, past other planets, past other stars; it kept going all the time. Space was full of light from all time. It only looked black up there if you didn't have the equipment to receive it.

He said in Egon they had the equipment built into everything. It was how the roads and buildings lit up; it was why the metal glowed. He said he had it on the submarine. He'd lit up the sea with it. He hadn't switched any lights on. He'd just activated the light in the sea.

I wanted to ask about the submarine; about how

he'd got it, and where he'd left it. But his mind was moving on. He said they had thousands of sciences, more sciences than I could imagine, like multi-gravity and anti-gravity. (That was how they kept the roof and the sea up.)

He said you didn't have to know all the sciences, but when you were old enough they fed you a few to see what your mind wanted. Until it was a hundred and eighty it hardly knew what it wanted, because it was still being made, and every mind was different.

He said though minds were all different, brains were all about the same. Brain was just basic stuff. It was like quartz or silicon that could be activated electrically; except what activated a brain was thought, which was faster. He said if you radioed a message to a planet three hundred light years away, it would *take* three hundred years. But if you did it on thought, the message got through immediately. He said all their messages went on thought. They had experts in their Thought Institute in permanent contact with space. Their brains were trained for it.

He said a brain was basically a computer that was programmed to make a mind and then act for the mind. It couldn't do anything by itself. For instance, when a baby was born it saw everything upside down. That's why it had such a dopey look. It was looking through its eyes, and eyes were lenses, and all lenses saw things upside down. One of the first things a baby had to do was tell its brain to put things right way up, and that way the baby's mind took charge of its brain and started growing.

He said once your mind was grown you could do what you wanted. You'd grown your life, your ego; you'd finally found out who you were. He said people above didn't know who they were, any more than ants did. Their minds were so small they had very little life, and even the bit they had they wasted. They mainly spent it swapping things with each other, and trying to get the best of a bargain, and then fighting if they got the worst of it. They never understood the point of their life.

I asked him what the point was, and he said I probably wouldn't get it but he'd explain a bit.

He said living creatures had minds, but all things had brains. A piece of wood had one. Wood was just millions of atoms all racing round in a certain pattern, and what kept the atoms in the pattern was what kept the wood being a piece of wood; otherwise it would turn into something else or fly apart. Things had to have brains; in fact, the world *was* one. The world was a single huge brain that kept all its separate brains in order.

He said though the world was a complete brain, it was still only a cell in another brain. The galaxy was a brain, too. It was one enormous whole brain, and worked like one, controlling all the millions of worlds that made it up, but it was still only part of another brain. The universe was a brain. And it even went further than that. Though the universe was a brain so gigantic that they hadn't even found a billionth of it yet, it was still only a bit of something else. It had to be. Brains were controlled by minds. There was a mind beyond the universe.

He was looking at me in a funny way as if he couldn't figure out if I'd got it yet.

I couldn't figure it out, either.

I said was this other mind God?

He said he hadn't done God yet so he didn't know,

but the universe was all controlled. All the million million galaxies were; all the billions of worlds were; every grain of sand was; and I was. That was the point of it, and it was why life was fun.

I couldn't see where the fun came in, but he felt around in my mind and said he'd try a bit harder. He said it was hard to explain fun. He said an ant couldn't understand it so it didn't have any. A rat understood a bit, and it had a bit. People understood more so they had more, and that's how it went. The bigger your mind, the bigger your life, and the more fun you saw in it. But whether you saw it or not, the fun was there. Life *was* fun. The idea of it was. The universe was, and you only had to look up to see it. It was an enormous game that kept going on, and you were playing in it; only people above hadn't glimpsed it yet.

Just then I knew I had glimpsed it. I remembered the feeling in the lake, that my life was somehow magic and part of a game I'd been playing without knowing. But I had no time to think of it. (I forgot to put we'd left the caverns by then. We'd checked out below, and checked out above, and he'd picked up the car. And he was still telling me things.)

He said people above would get the idea one day, but they had to get their minds bigger first; they had to live longer. They had to learn the medical science that would let them live first to two hundred and then three hundred, and everything would follow from that. He said their history had barely begun yet. And he started answering questions I didn't even know were in my mind.

He said no trace remained of their own history above because they'd gone below before the planet

114

looked as it did now. The mountains had worn down and built up half a dozen times since they'd gone below. He said the people had changed colour from brown to white because the sun's rays were filtered out by the receivers, and it had also turned their eyes green and their hair white. He said their space flights hadn't been detected because they used anti-matter shields, which you needed anyway at high speed to beat friction.

He told me so many things. And I wish he hadn't now. (I'll explain it.)

All I wished then was that I wasn't going.

He stopped the car at the point he'd stopped it when we came in, and I looked down the two miles and saw the sun was setting and everything had begun to glow.

The ragusas glowed, and the lake glowed, and the kites wheeled in the sky above.

I could hardly bear to leave it. I thought the fantastic things had all finished for me now; which shows how wrong you can be, for the most fantastic were just coming.

STRETCH
STRETCH

He wasn't speaking as we drove through the mountains. He drove fast, though it was dark now. The moon wasn't up. I looked through the open roof and saw stars in the sky, and looked at him, but he still didn't speak.

"What is it?" I said.

"I don't want you to go."

"I don't *want* to go."

"But I'll never forget you!" He blurted it out suddenly. "I want you to know that. You *won't* know it—after they've properly erased you. But you can know it now."

"How will I be erased?" I said.

"Specialists will do it. It's a big operation after all you've seen. They'll take out all you know of Egon. They'll take it out from the beginning, from when we met, and put something else in its place. They'll put planted memories in, to account for the missing time."

"What kind of memories?" I said.

"They invent them. They often bring people

down, to see what they know. Mainly they do it overnight and have them back in their beds again by morning. Or they get people wrecked at sea. They even let some of them stay a short time to get their reactions. But no one's seen as much as you."

"Can't any of them remember, when they get back?"

"None of them."

"Can they even dream of it?"

"You can't dream something that isn't in your mind. Nothing of Egon is in their minds. It won't be in yours, either."

He was silent a long time.

"Will *you* be taking me back?" I said.

"They're letting me. Though I wasn't supposed to go before."

Just then I remembered something I'd meant to ask before.

"What happened to the submarine?" I said.

"What submarine?"

"The one you brought me in."

The road suddenly lit up ahead. It lit up for miles like a long yellow snake. It did it automatically on dangerous roads when another car was coming. We'd left the pass between mountains now. We were on a track over a precipice, and he'd slowed. The other car appeared presently and passed, and the road faded into darkness again. I saw him peering over the side. Something was glimmering below.

"What is it?" I said.

"Lake Umbra. The deepest in Egon."

"What's in it?"

"Nothing. That's the point of it. It gives an idea of the abyss. I'll show you."

He stopped the car and fiddled with the dashboard, and we took off. We took off over the path and went down a few thousand feet to the lake.

It was a black lake, very still, between mountain walls. He pressed a switch and the car roof closed. Then we dropped into the water.

We dropped and dropped, in blackness.

"Can you feel it?" he said.

I felt something. Something was changing round me. "I can't see," I said.

He switched the light on.

The dashboard had moved. It had moved several feet ahead. It was still moving. It was twenty feet ahead, thirty, and still going. The whole front of the car was stretching. The sides were stretching, too. Ahead, a filmy substance appeared between us and the dashboard. It turned solid. Just while I was looking, it turned into a wall. The car doors were turning into walls.

I looked behind me and saw the back of the car had become a wall. And right the same moment, I realised the seat I was in wasn't a car seat any more. It was a easy chair. He was in one, too. We were at a low table. There was a carpet on the floor, and a sofa all along one wall. The room was about thirty feet long, and music began softly playing in it.

"Recognise it?" he said.

I was staring about, speechless.

"You asked about it," he said.

"Is this—the submarine?"

"It's a submarine, a car, a plane. It's my *vehicle*. It's programmed to do these things. It's just stretch mechanics."

We were still dropping. We were dropping fast. We must have dropped thousands of feet before he stopped the boat. He slid a panel from beneath the table, and pressed it, and the boat darkened and the wall lit up. Except, again, I saw it wasn't the wall but what was outside that had lit up. It hadn't lit up much. He pressed some more but it didn't light up any more. It stayed a mud colour, like fog.

"That's all the light in it," he said. "It never took in any more. It's heavy water. They bring kids here to give them an idea of the abyss. They can't show them the abyss itself."

"Why not?"

"They can't," he said abruptly. But all of a sudden he said a lot more. It seemed to shoot out of him as if he'd bottled it up and couldn't hold it any longer. He said he'd never get over how he'd killed me, or the pain I'd suffered. I started telling him I'd already forgotten it, but he wouldn't let me speak.

He said he *wouldn't* forget me: he kept saying it. He said he knew everything about me, and he liked me better than anyone in the world, and he couldn't bear to lose me, though he knew I had to go.

We just floated, a few thousand feet under water, and he kept talking. He said he wouldn't let a day pass without thinking of me. He said if he got through his exam the way he wanted, he wouldn't just think of me: he'd *be* with me. He started telling me about the exam and what he wanted to do.

He said it was mind communications. His grandfather was a director of the Thought Institute and had one of the minds they used for distant thought. He had fifty thousand lines in his mind and they

119

used them continuously, like a telephone exchange, even when he was asleep. The minds weren't only used for transmitting messages. They ran factories in space; they ran power lines for space energy; they navigated ships in space.

He said if he passed his exam, he'd do a year's preliminary and then another test to see if he was ready for the standard course. The course ran eighty years, then he'd go to university for another thirty years before starting mind communications.

I was slowly working it out. I worked out that if he did his preliminary, and then the standard course, and after it the university one, he'd be two hundred and ten before he started mind communications. I'd be a hundred and twenty-three by then! I'd be long dead by then! I asked how he thought he'd be able to "be" with me just after passing the first test.

He said the test wasn't anything. All you had to do was get on a thought wave with an examiner the other side of Egon. You got a flash in your mind when it happened. The examiner knew you'd be doing it, so you only had to get the time right. He said he could almost do it now, and my mind was so familiar he *knew* he could do it with me.

I asked if I'd know he'd be doing it, and he said I wouldn't. He said I wouldn't remember anything of him, not the slightest trace. And that made him so moody, he said he wanted to do something for me, something special, just to prove he'd never forget me. And suddenly he thought of it.

We were going up then. We left the lake, and he turned the boat back into a car, and we hit the road and started off again. But he was so excited he couldn't speak for a few minutes. Then he began nodding, and said he'd do it. He said it was an unbelievable thing but he'd do it.

I said, "Do what?"

He said, "Show you the abyss."

I asked what was so special about the abyss.

He said it was holy. He said there was no way I could imagine it. It was made of nothing. There was no air or gas or water in it, no energy, no time. But all life came from it, so it was holy.

I asked how I'd know it was holy if I'd been erased. He said he'd bring my memory back. He'd bring back the part I needed to know him. Then he'd show me the abyss, and it would prove he'd kept his promise, and he'd erase me again. He was sure he could do that, though he couldn't erase all I knew now. No single person could, and only specialists could do the operation, anyway.

I asked what kind of operation it was, and he shook his head. He said the problem was the knowledge was all over my mind now. The doctor at the lake had told him. A mind was so active that even if you took out ninety-nine per cent of it, the one per cent left could start remembering everything all over again. The specialists took *everything* out, and put back what they had to. And several of them did it together so they could check that everything went back in the right order and that the mind wasn't left mad.

He saw I was scared but he told me not to worry. He said he wouldn't leave me. He'd be with me all the time. And he wouldn't say goodbye before the operation just to prove we'd say goodbye after. We'd see each other after, and know each other after, and he promised it.

It didn't stop me being scared.

And it didn't help to look at him. I saw he was scared, too.

Even now I can't remember it properly. I've been trying, and I can't. I know it happened in the palace. I know I was on a couch, and that his father was there, and that five of them did it. But I'm not sure it's my own memory. I might have got it from his memory.

He was there: I knew that. The five of them and his father had moved away. But he was still standing beside me, and he said, "They're discussing the easiest way to do it."

I said, "Will I feel it?"

"I'm sure you won't. I'm *pretty* sure," he said. But his lips were dry, and he was licking them. "Anyway, I'll be with you. And I'll do what I promised. I'll keep nodding at you, so you'll know I'll keep the promise."

Then the specialists were back, and I was looking up at them, my heart thumping.

"Just relax," one of them said, and that's all I remember any of them saying. They'd bent over me and stared right in my eyes. And I was blinking up at them. I could see Dido behind, still nodding and licking his lips, and I licked my own, and waited for it to happen.

I just kept blinking.

I didn't stop blinking.

What happened must have happened in a blink.

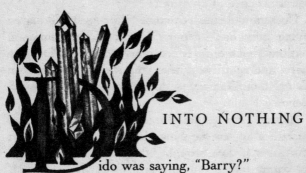

INTO NOTHING

ido was saying, "Barry?"

And I said, "Yes," and blinked round to see where the others were.

They weren't there any more.

I wasn't in the palace any more.

I was in the submarine. I was in the main room of it, lying on the sofa and blinking up at him. I couldn't think how I'd got here. I couldn't think *when* I'd got here.

He said, "Do you remember me, Barry?"

I said, "Of course I remember you."

"Do you remember the palace?"

"Of course I remember it."

"Do you remember Plum Lake?"

"What lake?" I said.

"*Plum* Lake. Have you heard of it?"

I hadn't. I'd never heard of anywhere like that. I felt confused. I kept remembering things and forgetting them again as if I was going off to sleep or trying to wake up. "Are we going there?" I said. I had an idea we were going somewhere.

123

"Not now," he said, and looked relieved. He felt my head. "I think I've done it right. . . ." He was looking at me closely. "Do you remember if I made you a promise of any kind?"

He had made me a promise. He'd been nodding to let me know he'd keep it. "Yes," I said, and hung on to it before it went. He'd promise to show me a place with nothing in it. There was something dreadful about it, and its name suddenly swam into my mind. "Abyss," I said.

"Okay." He licked his lips. "I'll do it, then. Barry—a lot has happened to you lately. You won't remember it. I've brought back just a bit. I hope it's the right bit. I mustn't interfere with the rest. They've put things in your mind that you'll need when you get back."

"Are we going back?" I said.

"We're going up. That's why—"

He stopped. A shuddering had started in the boat. He cocked his head as if listening. In the same moment I remembered having seen him do it before. And when he spoke I had a weird feeling he'd said the same thing before. He said, "Now. We're at it."

"At what?"

"The abyss."

He slid a panel from beneath the table and pressed it. There was a stronger tremor, like a high-speed elevator slowing, and he looked at me for a few minutes uncertainly. Then he touched a control, and the boat darkened and the sea lit up. It lit up for miles. He touched another control, and everything lit up. It lit up above, below, on all sides. I knew I'd seen this before, too, but with a difference. There was little to see now. All around was pale honey light and ahead of us a white mist. The mist seemed to be in motion, swirling.

I saw the boat had stopped, but it hadn't stopped shuddering. It shuddered like a jet before take-off.

"We have to go to the control room," he said.

I could see the control room: its panels and dials were glimmering ahead, as if in space. I seemed to be in space as we walked there; all the structure of the boat transparent now. I couldn't see the floor. I couldn't see the roof or walls. I just walked in space. The furniture hung in it. He turned left, then right, and the bathroom passed, and beds suspended in nowhere, and we were in the control room.

I could see the nose of the boat, nudging this way and that as if sniffing ahead. The wall of mist was ahead. It swirled for miles on either side, like a mountain range.

"Our own power's no use here," he said. "We go on thought to star power."

He pressed a button, and a screen above the cockpit lit up. It lit up with thousands of points of light. A circle appeared from the corner of the screen and began moving. It moved about the screen for a few seconds before stopping. It pulsed brightly for a moment or two and turned purple. Then the pinpoints of light that it ringed slowly faded, leaving just one, which turned purple and began to pulse with it. The pulsations fixed and beat together as the pinpoint began to expand. It expanded till it filled the circle exactly.

"Locked," Dido said. "They've got us. Now we have to lock ourselves."

There was a bench in the cockpit, and he sat me on it, and then himself. I don't know what else he did, but I was suddenly stuck. I couldn't move. "We'll drop a bit," he said. "Don't worry."

"Drop where?"

"Into the abyss. It's nothing. There *is* nothing. Don't worry," he said again. But I saw he was worrying himself. "You've got to forget this," he said quietly. "You're absolutely not supposed to see *this*!"

The boat had started slowly moving. It was moving towards the wall of mist. I saw now the mist was made up of enormous clouds, moving in a circular pattern, up and around, towards us. They seemed to be trying to push us back. Then we were in them, and wherever I looked there were clouds. They were a greyish white, and in furious motion, as if they were pummelling the boat, squeezing it. We seemed to be sliding and slithering through them as if on bumpy ice, and presently Dido said, "Hang on!" and we fell off.

We fell off the edge of something.

The nose of the boat dropped and the tail came up and we fell. We fell and fell, the boat toppling end over end. I could feel us falling and toppling but I couldn't see where. We'd fallen into total blackness. It was black outside, and black in. I couldn't see Dido, or myself, or even the dials. The dials had gone out. There was nothing at all to be seen.

Still weirder, we'd dropped into utter silence. There was no sound of any kind. In blackness and silence we tumbled and fell, and he said, "Barry, don't be afraid!"

I shouted, "I can't see!"

I shouted as loudly as I could, but no sound came out. And he hadn't made a sound either. He'd spoken into my mind.

"There are no light waves," he said. "There are no sound waves. There's nothing here. There's only thought. They've got us on thought — don't worry. They'll hold us and steer us through."

And as he said it, I felt us being held and steadied. And we were rising. We were rising and going forward, although still turning slightly; and again I felt a kind of vibration as if the boat was straining towards something and being pushed back. And he said, "Barry, if you see something, turn your head away. Don't look at it!"

"What is it?"

"The world creating itself. You mustn't see it, do you understand?"

"Yes."

But I saw it.

Just for a fraction of a second I saw it, and looked away but all the same felt blinded.

I couldn't believe what I saw. But the boat turned and I saw it again, and this time closed my eyes, and still saw it.

Behind closed eyes I could see it.

A gigantic pillar, shining like an iceberg, broad as a river, made of light. It was all of light, but it gave no light. It kept its light. All around was blackness. In the boat was blackness. The iceberg of light moved majestically upwards, a great molten mass, brighter than a furnace, brighter than the sun. Bits of it had crumbled off, and the bits moved upwards with it.

Behind closed lids, I felt my eyes searing. I felt my brain coming apart. I knew I was screaming, but no sound came out. I felt a hand on my head, and knew it was Dido's, and then everything went.

The terrible light went, and the blackness.

There was just his hand, on my head. And I was lying somewhere, and music was playing.

"Don't move," he said.

He was watching me.

I was on the sofa again in the main room, and the whole room was bobbing gently.

"What happened?" I said.

"We're back, in the world above. In your world," he said. He was bending over me, holding my head. "Look at me."

I looked in his green eyes.

"You saw it," he said.

"Yes."

"I'll take it away now. I'll take everything away."

"No. Dido—wait."

"I can't," he said. "I have to get you back. It's almost dawn there."

"Just for a moment—," I said, and found I couldn't say any more. My eyes seemed locked on his. There was a strange flicker in the green eyes, and a prickling sensation in my head. At the same moment I had a dizzy dream-like feeling that I wasn't me, but him watching me; and I was watching things in my head—things that flashed past like a speeded-up film. I knew it was me in the film, but what I was doing in it made no sense.

I was doing crazy things.

I was flying in a purple night.

I was watching a lake glow in the sky.

Then it wasn't a lake but a moat, and whales were racing round it, and I was racing with them. I was cascading in the air with the whales, and then they were in the sea below me; except the sea was a lake

128

of silver now, and there was a cliff in it with the black hole of a cave, and a little canoe bobbing in the moonlight. I was swimming to the canoe, and suddenly this was so familiar—the only thing familiar—that I shouted out loud. I shouted with all my strength, but it came out as a bleat, a shout from a dream. "Dido—stop there! I remember the canoe. What happened to the canoe?"

The flicker stopped in his eyes, and he paused.

"Well," he said, "I'll show you. Just for a minute."

He turned, and a door appeared in the back wall. "Can you move?" he said.

I said, "Of course I can move," but found I couldn't. I was weak as a kitten.

"You've got to feel like that," he said. "I'll help you."

My legs were so weak I could hardly stand. He got me to the door, and up some steps, and we were in the canoe, and I sat and looked round with amazement.

It was the same canoe. But it was in the wrong place. It was in the wrong time.

It had been the middle of the night when I'd got in it—just minutes before—and it had been bobbing by the cliff, in moonlight. Now it was in a vast sunlit ocean, and there wasn't a cliff in sight. There was nothing in sight.

"Where are we?" I said.

He pointed.

"Over there is China. And behind us, Australia. We're over the Marianas Trench, the deepest spot of the sea. Below it is the Glister Deep, and below that the abyss. You won't remember any of it."

I didn't. I didn't know what he was talking about.

And I didn't know what was happening to me. Even while he was talking I was forgetting what he said. I had the strangest feeling I was draining away. I had a feeling a lot of things had happened, and they'd happened with him. Yet I knew I'd only just met him. I'd met him in the cave. I'd gone down to the cave in the middle of the night, and I suddenly remembered I shouldn't have. I remembered I had to go back.

"I have to go back," I said.

"Yes, we'll go back."

"How long will it take?"

"Only minutes."

This was crazy. It was impossibly crazy.

"How long have we been gone?" I said.

"Three days."

"Three days! But—"

"It's all right. Everything is in your head. They've put it there. We've got to move now."

"But—my clothes," I said. He'd got me up and we were moving, and I'd suddenly realised I was wearing strange clothes. I was wearing a kind of tunic, with sandals. "Where are my jeans, the rest of my clothes—?"

"You'll have them," he said. "You'll be back in them. They're damp, but you'll find out why."

"And my watch. And the flashlight."

"The watch is okay. You'll find it going. The batteries in the flashlight wore out. You'll understand all this. You'll understand it on the shelf."

"Shelf? What shelf?"

He was stretching me out on the sofa. "There's no time," he said. "But, Barry, listen—I won't forget you!"

"I won't forget you," I said.

"You will. You're forgetting me already. You've forgotten my name."

I looked at him; and I had! I couldn't remember who he was. Moment by moment, it was all going.

"It's late," he said, "but I'll tell you something else. The specialists said—there were specialists but you won't remember—the specialists said you had a good mind. They said you had a good body. They said unless some accident happens, you'll have a great life. I'll see no accident happens. I'll try as hard as I can. I'll always watch you, Barry. I'll be your good angel. You won't know it, and there's no point in telling you. And you'd better settle down now." He had his hands on my head. "In a few minutes you'll wake up and hear it all start again."

"Wake up where? Hear what?" I said.

"Well," he said, and paused. And that's the last I remember of him. I remember the sea glinting behind him, and his head bent over mine. "You'll hear," he said, and he seemed to be listening, "you'll hear a kind of roaring sound."

Dream Journeys

THE PLANTED
MEMORIES

heard a kind of roaring sound. I'd heard every kind of sound the last few days of wind and gale. I turned on my side and looked towards the cave mouth. I was on a stone shelf at the back of the cave, chilled to the bone and aching all over.

It was lighter outside so I knew I'd slept a bit. It was a dirty grey light. Another day had come.

I tried to remember how many I'd been here. Was it three days or four? It was dark on the shelf, and I felt for the flashlight, and then remembered I'd tried it before and the batteries had given out. They had given out long ago. I swung my legs off the shelf, and felt my head swim again.

I was weak as a kitten. It wasn't so much hunger. That was just an ache now. The dizziness was worse. I felt dizzy every time I moved.

My feet touched ground and I stood and leaned against the shelf, waiting for everything to stop spinning. I wondered what I was going to do.

I couldn't jump up to the step on the cliff. I didn't have the strength; apart from climbing the cliff itself.

I'd had an idea I might wait for the storm to die, and take my clothes off and swim back. With the tide running, I'd float most of the way. Now I didn't have the strength for that, either.

It was a crazy thing I'd done!

I remembered coming down the cliff in the moonlight.

I remembered jumping off the last step and exploring the inside of the cave, and suddenly realising that the sea outside was becoming rough. I'd hesitated too long. Waves had begun slapping the step. They'd slapped everywhere. They'd started washing into the cave. The whole floor of the cave had become a pool, and I'd gone to the back and found the shelf there.

My clothes felt damp now. They'd been damp for days.

I'd known right away I was in trouble. After the first day I knew it was serious trouble. I thought I'd have to wait for the sea to stop pounding the step, and creep back, and take what was coming to me. But it had got worse. The sea hadn't stopped pounding. It had gone on and on.

My legs were so rubbery I didn't think I'd make it to the cave mouth. I thought I'd try it on hands and knees. But there were still pools of water everywhere.

I started lurching through the water. My head thudded at every movement, and even the murky light outside hurt my eyes.

But I could see it was different out there now. There wasn't the angry white flash of the sea. There wasn't the grinding sound of it pouring back off the cliff.

I went up the two steps to the platform and stood there a moment, swaying. I didn't dare go right to the edge. I thought I'd fall in. I just hung on to the side of the cave, and lowered myself into an inch of cold water. I was so exhausted I couldn't even bother getting out of it. I just sat there in the pool of water and looked at the sea.

It was the colour of lead now, with a sullen heavy swell. There was no white foam any more. I couldn't make out if it was coming or going. I couldn't make out the roaring sound, either. It wasn't the wind. It was hoarser, and sharper. It must be the birds. I'd heard them, too. During the storm some of them had fluttered into the cave before realising I was there; and then had fluttered out again, frightened. It was like bird noise, but different. The birds were calling in English.

With my head going round and round, I realised the birds were people.

I tried to get up, but couldn't. I just rolled forward on hands and knees. I must have looked like a dog there, a half-starved dog peering out of the cave. They saw me right away. And I saw them.

I saw the boat with the three figures in oilskins.

I saw one of them had a police uniform underneath, and another was using a long pole to keep the boat away from the cliff.

I looked hard at the other. I looked so hard my eyes swam and his head became two, and then one again. But both ways he was my father.

I remember the boat chugging slowly back to the cove, and them carrying me across the beach and up the rocky path. I remember a crooked ceiling and knowing I was in my own room again. Then a floating feeling, and I was in bed.

I heard Annie squeaking. She was squeaking, "Why has he got his watch on? Did he go swimming in it? Why has he got his clothes on? Did he go swimming in them?"

I wished she'd stop squeaking.

The room was full of people. One of them had a stethoscope round his neck, and was sitting on my bed, feeling my pulse.

Later my mother was there, alone, and she was giving me spoonfuls of soup. The soup was too hot and it was going down my chin.

She said I had to drink something from a glass. It was bitter and I couldn't get it down. But I tried a few times, and I did get it down.

I must have slept.

I had a dream.

I had the weirdest dream.

I was flying in a purple night.

THE BOOK OF
DREAMS

I don't want to write the next bit. I don't even want to think of it. They thought I was crazy. I thought I was, too.

My father didn't question me much. (They'd got him back from town when I was missing.) He hardly questioned me at all. They were very careful with me. They said I was delirious for days. I'd been yelling in my sleep, and sometimes even when I wasn't asleep.

After a couple of weeks we went back to town, but they still didn't question me. They just kept watching me. And at the end of the term I went to the doctor.

Nobody knew what was the matter with me.

I couldn't concentrate on anything. I kept looking out of the window. I had a feeling I'd lost something. I couldn't think what it was. But I couldn't think of anything else, either.

The doctor didn't find anything wrong with me, but he said I had to have some special tests.

I had the tests, and my mother took me back to him, and he asked when I'd broken my shoulder.

My mother said I'd never broken it.

He was looking at an X-ray, and he said I had. He said it was a beautiful job of resetting, and so well healed that it must have been done years ago, so maybe I'd done it as a baby and she'd forgotten.

My mother was so angry at the idea of her forgetting that he just laughed and said maybe they'd sent the wrong X-ray. But then he asked another thing. He asked why kites reminded me of death.

I saw he'd got my papers on his desk. They'd asked me questions during the tests, and I'd had to say the first thing I could think of.

I told him I didn't know.

He read a bit more, and then he looked up again and asked why darkness should remind me of an iceberg.

I said I didn't know that, either.

He brooded awhile and said he thought I'd better see one more specialist.

This specialist was a woman and she scared the wits out of me. I knew she'd heard about my being stuck in the cave, and my answers about kites and icebergs were right there on her desk. But she never mentioned any of them. She did it a tricky way of her own. She talked about being locked in cupboards, and about an air accident there'd been (a plane had blown up over the Arctic, killing everybody in it), and if I'd read anything about it.

I said I'd read a bit.

She asked if I dreamed.

I started saying no, but my mother said yes. She said I'd been yelling in my dreams.

The specialist asked what I remembered of them, and I said nothing.

She said the way to remember dreams was to keep a notebook and write them down first thing in the morning. She said you had to do it fast because they faded fast, and would I do that for her?

I said I would, but I knew I wouldn't.

I saw right away she thought I was crazy, so I wasn't going to give her the proof. I thought I'd keep the dreams to myself.

The notebook seemed a good idea, though, so I kept one. I kept one till I found my mother was reading it, and then I kept two. I kept one for my mother, by the bedside, and one for me, under the pillow.

I had a problem working out dreams for my mother. I ran out of old ones and started writing whatever I could think of. She didn't notice the difference, and when we went back to the specialist, she didn't notice it, either. But from the dreams I'd made up, she got an idea that was useful. She got the idea I was jealous of Annie.

The first thing that happened was that Annie got put to bed early. She was being a colossal pest just then, and she kicked up a row for days, but it didn't help her. They kept putting her to bed early. And the specialist's idea kept on being useful.

Annie knew about my dreams, and she used to come in the room early to see if I'd had one. She caught me once with the notebook I kept under the pillow. She didn't get the point of it, but it worried me, so I started being "jealous." I yelled that they let her do anything, that they let her come barging in my room, and that they thought more of her than they did of me.

That stopped her coming in, and Annie didn't

know why. She'd always come in my room. She couldn't understand why everyone was now picking on her, and all that happened was she got jealous of me. I was sorry about it, but I couldn't bother with her. I was too bothered by my dreams. I was having fantastic dreams. I was having more and more of them.

The one she'd caught me with was important. I'd had it in the middle of the night. I'd woken up sweating, so I knew I'd dreamed. I reached for the notebook without waiting to put the light on. I just wrote it in the dark, and put the notebook back and went to sleep again. I had another in the morning, and I was just adding it when she caught me.

The first dream was a problem. I could hardly read it. The writing slanted everywhere on the page. The words seemed to be: *Racing down Mount Julas. Window went over the side.* The second one read: *Sitting in a car and it starts stretching all round me.*

I could just remember that. I thought I'd had it before. I had a strange memory of being in something that started changing into something else. There was something familiar and dream-like about it.

Mount Julas was familiar, too, and I thought I must have read it somewhere. I couldn't understand the *window* that *went over the side.* I wasn't even sure it was *window.* The *w*'s were badly written. It could be *Dindor,* or *Dindo,* even *Dido.* The only clear letters were the *i,* the *d,* and the *o.*

I didn't bother with it, but I thought about *Mount Julas.* I thought about it all morning. I looked it up during lunch, in the school library. I found a Mount Julier in Switzerland, and a Mount Julijske in

Yugoslavia. There was a Julius in Alaska, and some other places, but there was no Mount Julas.

I didn't know what to make of it. I knew I hadn't invented it. I couldn't understand it. Just then I was having a bad time, anyway. I thought any day now the doctors would prove I was crazy, so I was trying to prove I wasn't. I was living two lives. At school I was acting normal, doing the best I could. I stopped looking out the window. I did all my homework. The rest of the time, I was thinking. I'd pretend to read a book or watch television, but I was thinking.

I'd had a fantastic idea. I had the idea the dreams weren't separate dreams. I thought they were one big dream, and that night after night I was having bits of it. Some of the bits were even repeating themselves! I'd be dreaming, and I'd know exactly what was coming.

And that wasn't all. I knew the trouble had started in the cave, but I could hardly remember it. There was nothing I'd done that I could properly recall. It was just a blur in my mind. Yet I'd been stuck there for days. I wondered what I *could* have done all that time.

I wondered if I'd hurt myself there, if I'd knocked myself out and had the dreams while I was unconscious, and that this was why I remembered the dreams but not the cave.

I couldn't believe that. It seemed ridiculous. Anyway I remembered the first dream I'd had, the one about flying in a purple sky. It had struck me as strange when I had it. I knew I'd never had it before. But I'd had it afterwards. I'd kept having it afterwards.

So I'd had the dreams *after* the cave; not in it, and

not before. Yet they obviously came from something that had happened while I was there.

I worried at it. I worked out all I'd done before the cave. I remembered taking the flashlight, and going out the window. I remembered finding the "rabbit hole," and the tunnel, and going down the cliff, and jumping off the step, and taking my clothes off. I couldn't think why I'd taken them off. I just knew I had.

The strange thing was, I couldn't remember putting them on again.

I thought about that. I went over it again and again. I wondered *when* I'd put them on again. I had an idea that if I worried enough I'd maybe dream it. And I did.

We were into the spring term. I woke up one night and knew I'd dreamed, and that I could remember it easily. I didn't even bother reaching for the notebook. I just lay there in the dark and thought of it.

I remembered jumping in the cave and seeing the hole in the floor, with the chain attached to the rungs. I'd had a feeling I had to try the chain. I did it, and found I had to take my shoes and socks off. I took everything off. I took off my watch and my windbreaker and pullover, then the rest, and wedged the flashlight near the hole, and just then a light shone back at me.

I said, "Who's there?"

He said, "Who's there?"

A kid came out of the hole. He had nothing on.

I said, "How did you get there?"

He said, "How did you get there?"

It went on. It just kept going on, in the dark. We went into a flooded tunnel. It was emerald green in the tunnel. I saw my hands big and pink in front of me. I saw a barrel and a box, both painted with tar, suspended and bobbing from the chain. We ducked under them. We went out to the sea, and a canoe was there, and we swam to it. It was a little canoe, six or seven feet. All around the breeze was wrinkling the water. He said, "Come and dry off," and went to the end of the boat, and I followed. We went down steps and he opened a door.

It was a room about thirty feet long. There was a carpet on the floor and a sofa all along one wall. There were easy chairs and a low table, and music was softly playing.

In my own room now, I was scarcely breathing. I was afraid the dream would vanish. But even then, with a mixture that was half fright and half relief, I felt something else.

I felt I hadn't dreamed.
I felt I'd remembered.
I felt it had happened.
Could it have *happened*?

GOING BACK

I couldn't think of anything else. I knew I had to go to Polziel. I had to go into the tunnel and see if there was a barrel and a box there.

I knew I hadn't been there before the night of the storm, and I'd not been since. I'd never even known about it except from my "dreams." If it was there, if *the barrel and the box* were there, then I hadn't dreamed it. Then it was real, and all of it was real.

I couldn't believe it. I couldn't even understand it. Night after night, day after day, I kept trying. And just then we had exams.

I did badly, of course. I did so badly, they thought of throwing me out. My father went up and saw them at school, and they said they wouldn't throw me out, but I'd have to do extra holiday work.

I didn't care about that. I couldn't care about anything. All the time now I was figuring out more. I found I couldn't "force" it: I couldn't deliberately try and figure it out. I got it wrong when I did. I dreamed once I was in a rocket and I saw earth and

146

knew I was in space. I tried to push it further. I tried to see what happened next. Once before, I'd dreamed of being in a place where fish swam in air and angels played harps on clouds. I thought that's what happened next. I thought I'd landed on a planet where they did that, and I forced myself to remember how I got there, and couldn't.

(I put that to show the difficulty. The dreams were coming in a crazy order, in snatches. It didn't help to go through my "dream book." I couldn't put the dreams together.)

I decided just to let the dreams come. I'd go to bed and lie there waiting. I'd say to myself, I am going to dream now. I am going on a dream journey. I must have gone on twenty journeys before we took off for Polziel.

I knew my parents were worried, and I was bothered they'd be watching me all the time at Polziel. But that worked out, too. My father said I had to do the holiday tasks in the morning, and nobody was to disturb me; so right away I took advantage of it.

Right after breakfast, the first day, I was back in my room. Inside five minutes I was out of it again. I went out the window.

I took a flashlight. I looked round to see no one was watching, and started off for the cliff. I was trembling so hard my legs shook. I got to the cliff and heard myself breathing a strange shivery way. I thought I was going to be sick. I thought I wouldn't find the hole. I thought I'd imagined it, and there wasn't a hole.

But I hadn't imagined it. The hole was there. Even the bits of slate I'd taken off the top were still there, exactly where I'd left them, almost a year ago. I just looked at them, and licked my lips, and shone the flashlight in the hole, and went down.

The hairs rose at the back of my neck as I swung the flashlight round. Everything as I remembered! There was the doorway into the tunnel. There was the gun lying where I'd dropped it. There was the breeze still sounding like someone blowing a bottle.

I started down the tunnel, and got to the blank wall, and poked the flashlight round, and followed it, round and round, till I came out to daylight and the west face.

There was the path again, zig-zagging down; and the birds flapping up in alarm, and the last step far below, with the wrinkled sea beneath it.

I started down right away, my heart banging. I slipped on the first few steps, and remembered how I'd done it before, and did it the same way, on my behind. At the last leg of the zig-zag I got to my feet again, and reached the bottom step, and just for a moment wondered how I'd get back. But I couldn't care about that, either, so I jumped, and landed on the platform, and in one glance took in the lot.

There were the two steps down to the cave, and the stone shelf at the back, with the old flashlight still on it. There was the barrel of hard tar secured to the wall; and the hole in the floor. . . .

I went to it immediately, saw sea water at the bottom, and stripped off. I went down the rungs, gasping at the chill, and took a breath and ducked.

It was pitch black there and I couldn't see a thing.

But I felt the chain dangling where I knew it would be, and pulled myself along it.

After a few yards the blackness wasn't so black.

There was a blur ahead, the color of pea soup. Daylight filtering through the sea. The end of the tunnel was ahead.

Something was bobbing in front of it.

Two things were bobbing.

I didn't have to go any farther, but I went. I felt them. I felt the barrel and the box.

I felt the smooth tar painted all over them, and turned and went back.

It was black all the way, this way, no light at all. I couldn't see where the tunnel ended. I just kept reaching up, and found the rungs, and climbed out.

I dried myself with my jeans and put them on, and went out on the platform and reached for the step. I hauled myself up easily. I'd grown this year. I went back up the cliff on hands and knees, and got to the tunnel, and went through it, and up the steps and out of the hole.

I didn't want to think yet. I was trying not to.

I was looking for a bigger piece of slate to cover the hole when I was suddenly sick.

I was sick as a dog, all over the grass.

I crouched on hands and knees, trembling, and couldn't help myself then. I thought of it.

I thought that all year nobody had known what was wrong with me, and I knew now. I thought that all year I'd felt I'd lost something, and I knew what that was, too, now. I'd lost a world.

I stayed there a few minutes, recovering, and then went home. I listened awhile to make sure they were all at the front, and I went in the back. I climbed up the post, and over the slates, and into my room, and sat there all morning, looking out the window.

A fantastic thing had happened to me that had not happened to anyone else in the world, and I didn't know what to think.

I couldn't tell anyone. It wouldn't help if I did, and I didn't have enough to tell, anyway. I had a few pieces of a jigsaw that needed hundreds of pieces. I didn't know where to put the pieces I had.

I wasn't the only one who'd been to the other world. He'd told me that. But I was the only one to remember it, and I wondered why.

That's what I thought in the end. I thought: why?

I thought it all week. I was like a zombie all week. I didn't hear what people said. I didn't know when it was mealtime. I couldn't eat at mealtime. (That's when they started talking of doctors again.) I kept thinking: why? And I kept dreaming.

I knew they weren't dreams now. I had them by day and by night. I had them everywhere. Mainly I had them in the cave.

I cleaned up the cave, and started clearing the steps. I went there and back through the flooded tunnel. One day I went to the library in Penzance and looked up Polziel. It said the place had been a fishing port, and the little harbour had been destroyed in a storm in 1790. Nothing was known of where the people had gone (except they hadn't fallen in the sea and weren't ringing any church bells there). Also they hadn't gone to Seele, because a centuries-old feud existed between the two villages. The villagers of Seele had always accused Polziel of smuggling. They accused them of wrecking ships for their cargoes of brandy and tea, though customs officials had found no evidence of it.

The same night I went down again and inspected the evidence. I did it in darkness. I felt the barrel and the box. I felt the tar painted over them and knew it was there to keep the contents safe under water. If I hadn't been under water myself I'd have laughed, because at last I'd found something about a place that no one had found before.

But even when I came out of the water I didn't laugh.

I sat in the cave and looked at the moonlight.

I looked at where I'd seen his canoe first.

"Dido," I said aloud. "Why did you do this to me, Dido?"

Then I knew it would happen again. I knew it would have to happen.

MAKING IT HAPPEN

Polziel, Cornwall, August 28.

Time's short now. We go back in three days. He knows that. He knows all I know.

He knows he shouldn't have done it.

He shouldn't have got me in the first place, and he shouldn't have brought my memory back, even for minutes. A mind is so active (this is what he told me) that even if you take out ninety-nine per cent of it, the one per cent left can start remembering all over again. And it happened. He did it wrong, and it happened. I remember what I'm not supposed to remember. And I don't want to. I don't want to know it.

I know the future is wonderful, and the idea behind it is, and life is. But I want to get on with my own!

Yet I want to see his again! I want to see the mountains in the sea and the canyons and the millions of fish. I want to see Plum Lake and the tigra forests and the glowing buildings of Egonia. I want to see it all just once, and then have it taken away. He said they brought people down overnight and had them back in their beds again by morning; and I want him to do it for me.

I know he'll be my good angel, and watch me all my life and "be" with me. And he is. He's in my mind now—I feel him. And I feel him watching, in the same way I felt him last year. He's out there somewhere.

So I've done it now. I've written it, and he knows it. He can't leave me like this. He has to come and get me—if only to get what I've written. Every night now I go down and tell him so.

I say, "Dido, you can't leave me like this." I say, "Dido, I'm not in my time, and I'm not in yours." I say, "Dido, you have to come and get me." I just keep saying it, as I'm saying it now. I say, "Dido!" I say, "Dido . . ."

ABOUT THE AUTHOR

LIONEL DAVIDSON is the author of seven previous novels—*Night of Wenceslas*, *The Rose of Tibet*, *The Menorah Men*, *Making Good Again*, *Smith's Gazelle*, *The Sun Chemist*, and, most recently, *Murder Games*. He lives in London.

SPECIAL MONEY SAVING OFFER

Now you can have an up-to-date listing of Bantam's hundreds of titles plus take advantage of our unique and exciting bonus book offer. A special offer which gives you the opportunity to purchase a Bantam book for only 50¢. Here's how!

By ordering any five books at the regular price per order, you can also choose any other single book listed (up to a $4.95 value) for just 50¢. Some restrictions do apply, but for further details why not send for Bantam's listing of titles today!

Just send us your name and address plus 50¢ to defray the postage and handling costs.
